D0971687

80470

jFic
SKU   Skurznyski,Gloria
      Swept in the wave of terror

DATE DUE			
MAR 1 '86			
JUL 27 87			
JUN 15			

"BOOKS MAY BE
RENEWED BY PHONE"

Swept in the
Wave of Terror

Swept in the Wave of Terror

GLORIA SKURZYNSKI

Lothrop, Lee & Shepard Books/New York

Mountain West Adventures
by Gloria Skurzynski

Lost in the Devil's Desert
Trapped in the Slickrock Canyon
Caught in the Moving Mountains

First Edition
1 2 3 4 5 6 7 8 9 10
*Designed by Sheila Lynch; photos courtesy Las Vegas News
Bureau; standard diver's signals drawn by Martha
Stoberock.*

Library of Congress Cataloging in Publication Data
Skurzynski, Gloria.
    Swept in the wave of terror.

    Summary: A brother and sister in Las Vegas are
caught up in a terrorist scheme to damage Hoover Dam.
    1. Children's stories, American. [1. Terrorism—
Fiction. 2. Las Vegas (Nev.)—Fiction] I. Title.
PZ7.S6287Sw 1985   [Fic]   85-4278
ISBN 0-688-05820-5

The author thanks Andrew and Lauren Thliveris for sharing their scuba expertise; Mary Jane Graesser for her horse expertise; Jack Drummond for his explosives expertise; and Janice Dixon for the use of "Child of Corn."

Special thanks go to the following people in Las Vegas for all their help: Heather and Bob Payne for the day spent on Lake Mead in the *Jolly Robert;* entertainer Peter Anthony; Janet Ford of the MGM Grand's *Jubilee!;* Phil Ronzone, Don Martinez, and Andy Anderson at the Tropicana's *Folies Bergere.*

I'm warmly grateful to Myriam Hernandez Gaete for playing the role of Ernesto with such enthusiasm.

For permission to use a variation of Evelyn Eaton's poem on page 84, I thank the Bear Tribe of Spokane, Washington.

STANDARD DIVER'S SIGNALS

For Andrew Thliveris

Swept in the
Wave of Terror

One

The two quarters in Tonia's hand felt wet from sweat.
Not because the temperature was so hot for May—
already a hundred degrees—but because Tonia had run
in a detour to the ice cream machine. She didn't need
to waste time making a choice; she wanted a plain,
ordinary, chocolate-covered ice cream bar on a stick.

With speed that came from lots of practice, Tonia
slammed quarters into the slot, pulled the knob, and
caught the ice cream bar before it hit the machine shelf.
Other people might have trouble peeling wrappers from
frozen chocolate; Tonia did not. After eating the bar in
six quick bites, she allowed herself a few extra seconds
to lick broken bits of chocolate from her fingers. The ice
cream, hanging suspended in the middle of her stom-
ach, radiated uncomfortable coldness because she'd
eaten it too fast. But she had to. The sign outside the
wire fence said in big, definite letters: NO FOOD OR
DRINK IN POOL AREA. And she had to get her
brother.

Inside the fence, Tonia walked to the edge of the deep

end and looked down. Through ten feet of water, she could see her brother Tiger clearly. Her heart gave a lurch that had nothing to do with the coldness of the ice cream inside her.

Tiger was lying on his back on the bottom of the pool. His blond hair, his arms, and his legs waved slowly, lifelessly, like seaweed. No air bubbles rose from the regulator beneath his face mask—Tiger wasn't breathing.

Just as the scream inside Tonia's chest was about to rip out of her throat, Tiger exhaled. A whole blob of bubbles skittered up through the clear blue water to explode on the surface.

The little whack! Playing dead to scare her out of her mind! Mad, relieved, and at the same time wanting to laugh because he'd scored one on her, Tonia thrust her arm into the water, elbow deep. She gave Tiger the "come up" sign.

She waited for him to come up, but he didn't. No one else was around, except at the shallow end of the pool where Heather, the lifeguard, was busy teaching a couple of preschoolers to blow bubbles with their faces in the water.

"Hi, Heather!" Tonia called, and Heather waved back.

If Heather hadn't been working with the tiny kids, Tonia would have asked her to swim underwater and yank Tiger up to the surface. By the hair, if necessary. It was Heather who'd taught Tiger to scuba dive. He was her best pupil, she said. Of all the people she'd taught, Tiger had caught on quickest.

12

Once more, Tonia put her hand in the water to make the "come up" sign, but Tiger ignored her signal. Ordinarily, Tonia could control her brother by making him laugh. She'd been pulling funny faces at him since he was two and she was three, and even now, ten years later, he still cracked up at them. From the bottom of the pool, though, Tiger couldn't see Tonia's facial contortions.

"But there are other ways to make you laugh," Tonia murmured, imitating a villain in a spy movie.

.   .   .

Tiger lolled in the deep water, relaxing, enjoying himself, imagining that he was Jacques Cousteau. He knew his sister was up there waiting for him by the side of the pool. Ten feet of water might blur vision so much that he could barely see an ordinary person's outline, but Tonia's shape was unmistakable. Tiger had recognized her in time to pull the breath-holding trick, which he hoped had scared the spit out of her.

Lying face-up was neat, although the air tank in his backpack didn't feel especially comfortable beneath him. Tiger liked to look up, through his face mask, through the clear, filtered pool water, up to where flecks of bright Las Vegas sunlight caught in ripples on the pool's surface. Things looked different from underneath a couple of tons of water.

Suddenly Tiger's eyes opened wide. Overhead, a frogman had begun to swim across the surface of the pool. He wore a vivid blue wet suit, and his mask, regulator, and air hoses were bright yellow. With his arms straight in front of him, the frogman rocked from side to side

13

as he swam, and his yellow swim fins made little "ploop ploop" splashes that Tiger could hear all the way down at the bottom. More startling than the sudden appearance of a frogman in the condo pool was his size. He was only ten inches long.

Tiger couldn't help it; he had to laugh. No matter how hard he tried not to, that plastic, battery-operated, flipper-kicking miniature frogman broke him up. There was no way Tiger could keep his face straight.

As soon as he laughed his cheeks crinkled, breaking the seal around his mask. Water rushed inside the mask to fill his nose and sting his eyes with chlorine. It felt awful. Clearing the mask underwater would be impossible while he was laughing, so Tiger surrendered and kicked up to the surface.

"Oh, hi," Tonia said casually when her brother's head broke through the water. "Mother sent me to bring you home for dinner."

.   .   .

"I can't believe it," said Mona, their mother. She stood with her right foot on the floor and her left foot high in the air, above her head. Mona could stand that way, with her leg straight up, for two whole minutes if she wanted to. And not lose her balance. It kept her muscles flexible, she said. Dancers needed to be flexible.

"Believe what?" Tonia asked.

"Believe what?" asked Tiger, who still had beads of swimming-pool water on his bare skin.

Their mother's left foot came down with a bang. "Casey!" she called to their father. "Come here and

14

listen to this letter that just came from your mother. You'll never believe it."

"Believe what?" their father asked as he walked into the living room.

Tonia and Tiger waited to hear. They couldn't imagine what their grandmother O'Malley might have written that was so hard to believe. Grandma was a pretty ordinary woman.

"She's not coming!" Mona cried, waving the letter as if she wanted to shake the words right off the page. "Your mother doesn't intend to spend the summer with us this year. She's met a man."

"I don't believe it," Casey said.

Tiger and Tonia looked at one another. If their grandmother didn't come to stay with them, everything would change that summer.

Their parents, Casey and Mona, worked from six in the evening until two in the morning, and slept till noon each day. That didn't matter when school was on: Tiger fixed cold cereal every morning, while Tonia warmed muffins in the microwave and poured orange juice for both of them. They ate hot lunch in school, and always came home to a delicious dinner—their father loved to cook.

In the evenings Mrs. Giles, who lived in a trailer court half a mile away, came to keep them company—Tonia objected to the word "babysit"—until their parents returned at 2 A.M. For a show-business family, it was a normal kind of life.

During the summers, though, Mrs. Giles vacationed

15

in Montana, and Grandma O'Malley came to stay with them for the whole three months that school was out. At least she always had. But according to the letter, Grandma O'Malley wasn't going to come this year.

"She's met a man?" Casey asked, grabbing the letter from Mona. "What kind of man? My mother's too old to be interested in men."

"Casey, she's only fifty-four," Mona answered. "The letter doesn't say much about him, except that he's a nice gentleman a few years younger than she is. She wants to stay in Cleveland to give the relationship time to develop."

"The relationship?" Casey's voice sounded as though someone were squeezing his neck. "My mother wants to develop a relationship with a younger man?"

"She's been a widow for ten years, Casey. She's probably lonely."

"She has us, doesn't she?" Casey yelled. "Besides, most women her age would welcome the chance to spend three months every year in Las Vegas."

Mona lowered herself into the Scandinavian modern chair and crossed her long, beautiful, smooth, tanned legs. "Grandma's never really approved of Las Vegas," she said. "Or of us being in show business. She only came here summer after summer so she could spend time with Tiger and Tonia."

"Yeah, you're right about her not liking show business," Casey said. "Look what else is in the letter. She didn't even appreciate the autographed picture of Wayne Newton we sent her. Listen to this—she says, 'I don't want Wayne Newton on my mantle,' " Casey read

16

aloud. " 'I would like some recent pictures of Tonia and Tyler. Please send some soon.' "

When Casey's tongue got twisted on all the s's, Tonia made a face that cracked up Tiger, which got their father even madder.

"Cut it out, you two. Tiger, quit dripping on the rug," Casey yelled, as if Tiger's dripping had anything to do with the real problem.

Pretty soon it's going to hit him, Tonia thought. Right now Dad's mad about a lot of things. But soon he's going to zero in on the fact that since Grandma isn't coming, Tiger and I will be all alone all summer.

She started counting the seconds, sure that in about one minute her mother or her father would explode, "Hey! What will we do with the kids?"

Thirteen, fourteen, fifteen . . . "What about the kids?" they both asked at once.

Tonia was ready. Before her parents had a chance to answer their own question, she plunged in.

"You don't have to worry about us," she said. "Tiger and I can stay here by ourselves. I'm thirteen, for holy sakes! Lots of girls my age take care of other people's kids. And Tiger's twelve, even though he only looks eight."

Tiger winced.

"We're trustworthy," Tonia went on, rushing the words as her voice grew higher. "We're reliable. We're clean in thought, word, and deed. We'll go to bed on time, and we won't watch any explicit movies on cable TV."

Tiger looked revolted at the very thought of such a thing. "Yuck," he said, sticking out his tongue.

17

"Impossible," their mother said.

"No way," said their father. "We're not leaving you two kids alone here night after night until the wee hours of the morning. We'll scout around and find another babysitter."

"Babysitter!" Tonia cried. The word was too humiliating. At least when Grandma stayed with them, no one could call her a babysitter. She was just a visiting grandma.

"Maybe Heather could tend us," Tiger said, hope in his eyes. Tiger was sort of in love with Heather, and she thought Tiger was adorable. Everyone thought Tiger was adorable.

"I doubt it, honey," Mona answered. "Heather already teaches scuba at the university and works here at the pool, too. I'm sure she couldn't handle a third job."

The phone rang, interrupting the discussion, and Mona went to answer it. Casey frowned in concentration as he listened to Mona's end of the conversation, trying to figure out what the person on the other end of the phone might be saying. At the same time he sniffed to make sure his casserole wasn't burning.

The pause gave Tonia time to grope for a solution to their problem. How was she going to prevent some stupid stranger from babysitting them all summer? She reached for a handful of Hershey's kisses to increase her mental energy.

No one told her not to eat the candy. No one ever told her to cut down on the large amounts of food she consumed constantly. "She'll outgrow that pudginess when she reaches puberty," Mona always assured people.

Tonia wasn't certain what Mona considered puberty to be. As far as Tonia knew, she'd already reached it, a few months earlier. But she was still pudgy.

The main temptation was Casey's fabulous cooking. At that very moment, their condo was filled with the marvelous smells of whatever fancy recipe he had in the oven. As soon as Tiger dried off and put on some clothes, Casey would take out the casserole and set it on the table with a flourish. He loved to fix rich, delicious dishes for the whole family, dishes that Tonia ate most of, because Tiger was a picky eater and Mona and Casey were always dieting—dancers had to stay slim.

Mona dieted even more strictly than Casey. She'd make a big to-do over every luscious plateful he cooked, sniffing the aroma, groaning about how exquisite it looked and smelled. Then she'd take one or two bites, and push her plate toward Tonia, saying, "Here, finish this, honey, so it won't go to waste. Someone ought to enjoy it." The food never went to Mona's waist; it went to Tonia's.

Her overeating made Tonia feel guilty. As she watched Tiger pick at his plate while she porked out on her own food, Tonia would yell at him, "If you'd eat more, you wouldn't be so short."

"Let him alone. He'll shoot up when he reaches puberty," Casey always answered. Their parents seemed to think that everything wrong with Tonia and Tiger would magically disappear at puberty.

Mona said goodbye to whoever was on the phone, and gently lowered the receiver into its cradle. "I'm afraid to believe it," she said.

19

"Believe what?" all three of them asked.

"That was Ben Bass. He's casting a new show. He wants us to audition."

"I'm not sure I want to leave the show we're in—" Casey began, but Mona stopped him.

"Wait! Let me tell you what he said. This might be the answer to our problem." Mona looked so cautiously excited that Casey took her hands; they sank together onto the loveseat. They made a beautiful couple.

"It's a brand-new concept in Las Vegas entertainment," Mona said, a little breathlessly. "A family show. G-rated. One that parents can bring their children to."

Although Mona was speaking to Casey, Tonia and Tiger settled on the floor near them to hear everything. They knew Ben Bass, the producer. He'd come to dinner at their home lots of times. They listened with interest as Mona told what Ben had said.

It seemed the owners of the new WestAmerica Hotel, which had no gambling casino—only rooms and restaurants—wanted to provide wholesome live entertainment for families vacationing in Las Vegas. The show, if things went according to plan, would begin at seven each evening and end at eight-thirty, so that children in the audience could be put to bed on time. It wouldn't be just a kiddie show; it would provide good, solid entertainment for grown-ups as well.

"I told him we'd probably want to audition," Mona went on. "And then—I don't know what made me say it, maybe an impulse from heaven—I asked Ben, 'Will there be any children in the cast?' And Ben said he was considering it. Then I asked, sort of hesitant, 'Could

Tonia and Tyler try out?' Ben didn't answer at first, but finally he said, 'Sure, why not? Bring them along when you audition.' " Mona beamed. "Isn't that wonderful? If all four of us get parts in the new show, we wouldn't have to leave the children. We could all be together."

"Mo-o-o-ommm!" Tonia moaned. "I don't want to be in a show. Besides, I'd never get past the audition."

"Oh, sweetheart . . ." Mona turned from Casey to focus on Tonia. "You wouldn't have to sing or dance. You'd just be background, like the scenery."

"Mom, no one wants an ugly fat girl—"

"Now, I won't hear any of that kind of talk. You're going to be just beautiful, as soon as you reach puberty. And darling, you know what my dream has always been."

Mona and her dream—wasn't she ever going to give it up? Tonia couldn't remember when she'd first heard about Mona's dream; she was so young that she thought it was something her mother had actually dreamed at night, in bed. Not till Tonia grew older did she realize that the dream was a daydream, a longing, Mona's motherly fantasy.

Mona had begun dancing professionally when she was seventeen. She'd had Tonia when she was twenty. If Mona could keep herself in peak physical condition until she was thirty-seven—the absolute outer limit, the oldest a female dancer could hope to perform in a top-rated Las Vegas production—by then Tonia would be seventeen. It was Mona's dream that she and her daughter appear together in one major show. "If that happens, I'll retire happy," she always said.

But it wasn't Tonia's dream. Tonia hated her dancing lessons—she looked horrible in a leotard. She hadn't been born beautiful like her mother. And her father. And her brother. Especially her brother.

Tiger looked like an angel—everyone said so. His hair was as soft and yellow as a newborn chick. Long dark lashes fringed his big, blue, wide-apart eyes. Two deep dimples appeared in his perfect pink cheeks whenever he smiled, and his smile melted people. Total strangers. Even his shortness was an advantage: people thought he was much younger than twelve, so they tweaked his cheeks and tousled his hair and gave him quarters for lollipops.

When Tonia complained of her ugliness, compared to Tiger, her mother said, "Don't be ridiculous. You have exactly the same features as your brother."

That was true, in a way. Tonia was blond, too, but her hair had the hue of a sun-scorched newspaper left on a rooftop too long, and it drooped lifelessly around her head like wilted cabbage.

Her blue eyes were shaped the same as Tiger's; she couldn't deny that. But they were set too close together. Her dimples got lost in the chubbiness of her cheeks. And her smile never melted anyone, because her lips went all crooked when she smiled. No sane producer would ever want Tonia in a show.

"Ye gods!" Casey said, "look at the time! If we don't eat right away, Mona, we'll be late for work. Tiger, go put some clothes on. Tonia, help me carry the food to the table."

22

Two

"Okay, everybody take a break except for all the boys. I want the boys to remain onstage," announced Jocko Pollack, the director.

"Does that mean I'm supposed to go onstage?" Tiger asked. "I'm a boy."

"No, stupid, he means the men dancers," Tonia told him. "Dancers are always called boys, or girls, or kids. It doesn't make any difference how old they are."

The twelve boy dancers—average age twenty-four—stayed onstage while the rest of the cast moved into the showroom. Tonia and Tiger had sat at a table in the showroom for most of the morning, waiting to be told what to do. It was the first week of rehearsals. Much to her own amazement, Tonia had been hired with her parents and Tiger as part of the cast. But the director hadn't yet figured out how to use her. Or Tiger.

"Whew! I don't know why they keep this place so cold," Mona complained, shivering as she reached them. She started to pile a sweat shirt, sweat pants and leg warmers over her tights and leotard.

"The air conditioning must be turned below sixty," Casey said. His head emerged through the turtleneck of a thick sweater. Like Mona, he had to stay warm so his muscles wouldn't stiffen. Since Casey was a principal dancer, not one of the chorus, he wasn't required on stage just then. He reached for the thermos of hot tea that Mona had brought.

"All right, boys, we're going to learn the opening number. The Indian number. Make a circle," Buzzy, the choreographer, told the chorus boys. Jocko Pollack sat at a table in the back of the showroom, where he could see the whole stage, and could direct through a microphone so everyone heard him. Next to him sat Ben Bass, the producer. Bearded Ben and bald, bespectacled Jocko sat detached, like God, from the rest of the company. It was the choreographer, Buzzy, who had hands-on contact with the dancers.

While taped music played through the sound system, the twelve boy dancers shuffled in an Indian circle dance: BOOM boom boom boom, BOOM boom boom boom. "Where's that little boy Tiger?" Jocko asked through the mike. "Tiger, you go up on stage and join the circle."

"Uh . . ." Casey looked at Mona, then at Tiger. Mona looked at Casey. Tiger looked uncertainly at both of them.

"You'd better go. Give it a try. Maybe it'll work," Casey whispered, and Tiger walked slowly onto the stage.

"Just dance the way the boys are dancing, Tiger," Buzzy told him. "You saw what they were doing, didn't you?" Tiger nodded, but he looked worried. As the tape-recorded drumbeat began again—BOOM boom boom boom, BOOM boom boom boom—Tiger began to move.

"Wait a minute. Something's wrong," Jocko muttered from the back—the mike picked up his mutter. "Buzzy, show the little boy what he's supposed to do."

"Uh oh," Casey said.

Mona sighed. "We'd better get it over with."

The two of them walked back to where Jocko and Ben sat. Tonia followed, curious to see how it would turn out.

"Look, Ben," Casey began, "Tiger wasn't hired as a dancer. He was hired just to stand around and look cute. Tiger's real good at that. No singing or dancing, though. Tiger can't dance."

"What dancing?" Jocko asked. "I just want him to go around the circle twice in that Indian shuffle. Then he'll move to stage left, out of the way."

"Tiger can't—"

"Casey," Jocko interrupted, "it's not dancing; it's just a dumb little shuffle. Anyone who can clap his hands in time to music can do that dance."

"Tiger can't clap his hands," Mona explained. "Not in time to anything."

Jocko looked at her in disbelief. "Don't be silly. Anyone can clap hands."

"Not Tiger," Casey said.

"You've got to be kidding."

Tonia and Tyler—their parents had chosen those names for the two of them because the names would look great on a theater marquee. Or a billboard, or a

25

printed program. Tyler and Tonia, the famous brother-and-sister dance team. A dance team that would never exist, because the Tyler part of it—also known as Tiger—had been born with no sense of rhythm.

Mona and Casey realized that terrible truth by the time Tiger was two. For months they'd tried to teach him to play pat-a-cake. "Bake me a cake as fast as you can," they'd repeat, stressing the tempo as they clapped Tiger's fat little hands together in rhythm. But whenever Tiger tried to do it by himself—and Tiger always tried hard to please—he couldn't get the beat. No pat-a-cake, no matter how old he got, because Tiger had absolutely no rhythm.

"How can he swim, then?" Casey often asked, because Tiger had taken to water like a duck. When Heather started teaching him scuba, Casey asked her the same question. "How can Tiger be such a good swimmer when he has no rhythm? Look at him flapping his fins down there!" Casey had pointed into the pool. "Don't scuba divers need to move their legs in some kind of rhythm?"

"Not necessarily," Heather replied. "They just have to move them one after the other—it doesn't require any special beat. Tiger isn't trying for speed or endurance, where rhythm would matter. He's just having fun at the bottom of the pool, and he's doing fine."

He did not do fine, however, in the Indian dance. "Take Tiger out of the line," Jocko ordered over the microphone so the whole company heard it. Mona blushed with embarrassment and Casey looked grim. Tonia gloated a little, but secretly. She really loved her

26

brother; it was just that people fussed over him so much, usually, that it did her heart good to see him publicly put down for once.

Sheepish, Tiger joined them when they went back to the bare-topped table that held their clothes and street shoes and Mona's knitting. The tables and chairs rested on tiers that curved into an amphitheater facing the stage. After the show opened—opening night was scheduled for August seventeenth—those tables would be covered with cloths and napkins, silverware and plates. The audience—mothers and dads and kids—would sit in the chairs and eat Western Bar-B-Q while they watched *The Way the West Began* onstage. And Tiger would sit or stand onstage and look right back at the audience, without having to dance. He smiled with relief, but tried to hide the smile, because his parents were unhappy with him.

"The number still doesn't look right," Jocko's electronic voice reported from the back. "It needs something more. Where's the little fat girl?"

Tonia tried to slip behind her father's chair where no one could see her, but Casey's hand reached back to pull her out.

Jocko murmured, "I apologize for saying that. The girl's name is Tonia, Ben has just informed me. Tonia, sweetie, would you kindly go onstage? I'd like to try something."

"Do I have to?" Tonia moaned, in a whisper, to her parents.

Mona's eyes danced. "Honey, this might be your big chance."

27

"Your chance to defend the family honor, after Tiger's less than noble performance," Casey said. He gave her back an encouraging pat and her arm a strong yank.

"I don't really want to do this. . . ."

"Tonia," Jocko's voice boomed. "Onstage, please. Move your tush."

If Tiger had walked onto the stage with reluctance, Tonia approached it with dread. She imagined every eye in the cast following her, everyone in the company wondering why on earth Jocko was sending that awful-looking girl onstage.

Jocko said, "It wouldn't look realistic for one little squaw to dance with the braves. So move Tonia to stage left, Buzzy. Back farther. That's it, right there. When the music starts, have her dance her own little shuffle dance in the corner by herself. Act as though you'd really love to dance with the big strong Indian braves, Tonia, but they won't let you."

Love to dance! All Tonia wanted was to be inconspicuous, invisible, home in bed with the mumps or something. She felt naked onstage as everyone looked at her. It wasn't fair that Tiger got out of performing while she had to make a fool of herself—dancing, yet! How awful she would look, with her plumpness jiggling up and down to the BOOM boom boom boom of the taped music. Tonia the Tub pretending to be an Indian.

"Okay, Tonia," Buzzy said, "let's try it. You do the same steps the boys are doing, but dance alone. Stay stage left. That's the way."

Tonia's sense of rhythm worked just fine; she'd

28

learned pat-a-cake at six months. She gritted her teeth and forced herself to do what Buzzy instructed.

"That's good!" Jocko yelled. "Okay, Tonia, you move into the wings as the circle of dancers parts. Boys, move back to reveal a figure in the center of the stage. Where's the old Indian? Chief, where are you?"

From a table in a corner of the showroom, where he'd been waiting in shadow, an ancient Indian stood up. As he walked toward the stage, moving with fragile care as though his bones might not be trustworthy, everyone could see that he was the real thing. His gray hair hung in two thick braids, one braid in front of each bony shoulder. The brown, leathery skin of his face had as many lines and seams and creases as a woven willow basket. Around the collar of his Western shirt—a plaid shirt with snaps instead of buttons—hung a bolo tie decorated with a piece of turquoise bigger than a silver dollar.

"Take your place center stage, Chief," Jocko told him. "As the circle of boy dancers moves apart, the audience will see you standing there with your arms raised in prayer. Then you say the Navajo poem. Say the words slowly, with feeling. Like this." Jocko demonstrated by reading the lines over his microphone:

> "Child of corn, I wander,
> In the earth mist, I wander,
> Beauty below me.
> With the turquoise sun, I wander,
> Beauty above me.
> With the pollen of dawn on my trail, I wander,
> Beauty before me.

Always in beauty, I wander.
I wander."

Jocko spoke the lines with so much feeling that at the end, his voice grew husky. "Beautiful! Beautiful sentiments," he said. "Now you do it, Chief."

From center stage, the old Indian raised his head. Tonia skittered to the front part of the stage wings and stood inside the leg, the side curtain that kept the audience from seeing backstage. From there, she could watch the old man's face.

His deep eye sockets looked like holes poked in sand by a burning stick. His eyes, little pieces of silky charcoal, peered intently into the shadowed showroom.

"Those are not the words of my people," he said.

"What do you mean? That's a genuine Navajo prayer, or poem, or something. I have it on the best authority," Ben Bass argued.

"Not my people." The Indian folded his arms across his narrow chest.

Ben and Jocko conferred, their muttering picked up by the mike. Tonia wondered if they knew that every word they spoke, no matter how softly, was audible to the whole company.

". . . maybe means he's not a Navajo. . . . Humor him. He looks absolutely perfect for the part."

"Uh . . . Chief," Ben said, speaking aloud, "if you don't want to say the Navajo prayer, why don't you give us a prayer from your own people?"

The Indian unfolded his arms, took a breath, and looked upward toward the high ceiling, up to where

30

fifty-two rows of pipe would raise and lower backdrops
once the show started. In chopped syllables, the old
man said,

> "Timpi Kadid,
> uabi witu'a;
> umpa'nitug
> noyu' kwaigig."

After a moment Ben remarked, not unkindly, "That
was very nice, Chief, but do you think you could trans-
late it for our benefit?"

Not understanding, the old man frowned.

"Say it in American," Tonia whispered loudly from
behind the leg.

"Can't say it in American. It has meaning only to my
people." The thin arms folded across the chest again,
and the gray head bowed with finality.

Through the microphone came more muttering.
". . . get a translator from the university. Work out
something with the old guy." Aloud, Jocko said, "We'll
figure out some way to do it, Chief. We'll have your
prayer translated. Our writers can fix up the words a bit
and maybe add a few lines to make it right for the
show."

The Indian dropped his arms and straightened his old
body. "No! I will not let you change my people's song!
Already too many changes in the ways of my people.
You took our land, our Mother Earth, and you changed
her. Drowned the heart of her with your big dam." He
gestured, but Tonia wasn't sure whether he pointed in

31

the actual direction of Hoover Dam—it didn't matter. The old man's words had riveted Tonia's, and everyone's, attention.

"Chief, would you please say that again?" Though Ben's request came softly and respectfully over the mike, Chief didn't repeat what he'd been asked to repeat. He said other things.

"Where my people hunted, your people spray paint across our sacred symbols on the rock cliffs. On our lands, you put flashing lights and naked women; you call it Las Vegas Strip. Strip! That's what you did—you stripped Mother Earth of her sacred garments."

"Wow! Did you get any of that down on paper?" At their table in the back of the showroom, Jocko and Ben whispered in excitement. "He's sensational! If we can work that into the finale, what an impact it will have!"

Except for Ben's and Jocko's low-pitched comments that the mike picked up, a hush had come over the company. Tiger began to move slowly toward the stage, not taking his eyes from the old Indian.

In the hush, Jocko sounded even louder. "Fine, Chief. We'll fix things so you're satisfied. You can come off the stage now. Everyone take an hour break for lunch. Be back here at two sharp."

The Indian hesitated at the steps leading down from the stage, not sure of his footing. In an instant Tiger was beside him to reach for his hand. After Tiger led the old man through the tables back to the corner where he'd sat earlier, Chief sank into a chair, looking frail and old. Tiger sank onto the floor next to him. Consciously or unconsciously imitating the old man, Tiger folded his

32

arms across his chest and gazed up at Chief, ready to offer him any further service he might need.

From the shadow behind a half-open door that led from backstage to the parking lot outside, other eyes studied Chief; dark, narrowed eyes that glittered with resentment.

Three

"Get down here on the floor with me and stretch your muscles," Mona told Tonia.

"Do I have to?" Tonia asked. It came out garbled because her teeth were stuck in a piece of toffee.

"Yes, you have to. You've been sitting there for an hour reading that teen romance. By now your muscles must have grown as stiff as dead fish." Mona touched her elbows to her knees, then to her toes. "Suppose Buzzy calls you to rehearse the Indian number. What are you going to tell him—'You'll have to wait, Buzzy; I need ten minutes to warm up'? Act like a professional, Tonia. Other girls your age would give their eyeteeth to be in a show like this."

Extracting her own eyeteeth from the toffee, Tonia grumbled and slid to the floor. "Tiger's lucky," she said. "He doesn't have to dance. He doesn't have to warm up. He hardly ever gets called onstage, even. All he does is sit next to Chief and yak all day."

Bending at the waist so that her left hand reached

over her head toward her stretched-out right leg, Mona asked, "What do they find to talk about?"

"Hardly anything. Tiger asks questions, Chief answers them. Oof!" Tonia's tummy got squeezed as she bent to touch her toes. "Only it takes Tiger about five minutes to—oof!—ask each question. And Chief answers—ugh!—in about two words, and then—ouch!— Tiger waits five more minutes and asks another question."

"Must be a dazzling conversation," Mona said. She was doubled like a jackknife, not even breathing hard.

"Principals onstage for the Spanish number," Jocko called over his microphone. Mona, nice and limber, hurried onstage with Casey and the six other principal dancers, while Tonia, who felt as though she'd been released from jail, scuffed toward the corner where Tiger and Chief sat.

"How many years have you been a chief?" she heard Tiger ask as she plunked down next to them.

"I'm not a chief. My people don't have chiefs."

Tiger thought this over. Tonia had exaggerated when she said that five minutes elapsed between Tiger's questions. It was actually only about one minute, but sixty seconds of silence can seem like a long time.

"Jocko calls you Chief," Tiger said.

Chief nodded.

"Doesn't Jocko know your real name?"

Chief shook his head.

Another pause. Then Tiger asked, "What is your real name?"

35

"Yanpa' vinuk," the old man replied.

The long pauses in the conversation were making Tonia fidget, even though Tiger had explained to her that being nosy—asking a whole stream of questions—was considered impolite by Indians. Why he thought that spacing out his questions was more polite than asking them all at once, she couldn't understand. The snail's pace of their conversation drove her hyper.

At last Tiger asked, "Yanpa' vinuk—what does that mean?"

"Runs-like-mockingbird," the old man answered.

"*Runs* like mockingbird!" A loud giggle escaped from Tonia. "Shouldn't it be *Sings*-like-mockingbird? Or Runs-like-a-deer? Whoever heard of a running mockingbird?"

Tiger squeezed his eyes shut as if he were unbearably humiliated. Speaking the way he thought Indians talked, Tiger said, "Please excuse my sister. Sister has much mouth, but not much brains. No manners at all."

Tonia lunged for Tiger and wrestled him to the floor. Since Tonia weighed a hundred and thirty-seven and Tiger weighed eighty-two, it was no contest. As Chief reached down to disconnect them, Jocko blared into the microphone, "What's the commotion over there?"

Tonia rolled off Tiger and sat up. "We're just doing our warm-up exercises," she said, opening her eyes wide to look innocent. It was a fakey excuse, but she hoped it would prevent a scolding from Casey and maybe win some praise from Mona. The way her parents glared at them from the stage, though, she knew she hadn't fooled anyone.

"Now you got us both in trouble," Tiger growled into her ear, but Tonia ignored him, pretending to watch the principal dancers rehearse.

After a while she didn't have to pretend—she really became intrigued, watching her parents dance. They were so good! Casey and Mona and the other principals followed the instructions of the choreographer, seeming to know instinctively what Madame wanted.

Madame Alejandra had been brought in as an additional choreographer to direct only the flamenco number, a dance that would show the Spanish influence in the West. Although she wasn't anywhere near as old as Chief, Madame was pretty old, Tonia thought. She had lots of wrinkles on her face.

Still, Madame seemed beautiful to Tonia. Her raven-black hair gleamed. Around the edges of her big dark eyes, around her mouth, and on her forehead, her wrinkles connected into a mask of smiles that seemed to say, "I have lived long. Life is pretty good, for the most part. But to dance! To dance is everything!"

"One! Only one strong beat with the hands and the feet," Madame called out in her rich voice. "One two, one two, one two three, one two three, bup ba BAH! Girls, reach up the arms to caress the clouds with the hands. Boys, with the heels, prove your manhood to the earth. Speak with the hands and the feet! Bup BAH! *Muy bién!*"

The dancers had practiced the flamenco all that week, the second week of rehearsals. They looked nearly perfect, Tonia thought, especially her parents.

Lithe and slender, Mona stood five feet ten inches

tall; in the two-inch heels she wore for the flamenco, she was the same height as Casey. Both had narrow hips, taut abdominal muscles, and a grace that made their bodies flow like water in a fountain. Watching them, Tonia felt pride surge up in her chest, the kind of bursting pride she felt when her school's team made a spectacular last-second shot on the basketball court. At a game, the rush of pride could bubble into a happy, excited cheer. In the rehearsal showroom, it could only catch inside Tonia's tight throat, to choke her a little as her parents' shoulders thrust up and down to the fiery flamenco music, as their hands clapped and their heels beat a tattoo on the stage.

"Casey!" Madame cried. "Don't collapse the elbows. Elbows must not flap like scissors. Mona! You should not lift the skirt as if you were shaking a dustcloth."

Tiger dug his fingers into Tonia's well-padded ribs. "Madame's yelling at Mom and Dad," he said. "I never heard Mom and Dad get yelled at before. It's funny."

"It isn't funny, you squid! If brains were dynamite you wouldn't have enough to blow your nose." Tonia scowled at her brother, resisting the urge to punch him for thinking it funny that their parents got scolded like naughty school kids. "Besides, Madame yells at the other dancers, too."

At that moment Madame was warning all of them, "It is of the most importance that you dance where you belong. If you move from your right place, the horse may kick you—should that happen, it will be catastrophe. Remember to take care, because now we bring on the horse."

"Horse? What horse?" Tiger asked.

"The horse that's going to be part of this number. Didn't you know there's a horse in the flamenco number? *I* knew that." Tonia turned to give her brother a superior look, and missed the horse's entrance.

A dark-haired, dark-eyed young man led the gray gelding through the door from the parking lot.

"Oooh!" Tiger jumped to his feet. "Look at it!"

As the young man, who didn't appear to be much older than a teenager, led the horse from right to center stage, another man—older, with thick black hair and a haughty lift to his head—crossed from left to center stage. The older man wore tight-fitting black trousers, a silver shirt unbuttoned to his belt, and gray snakeskin boots. Moving so quickly that Tonia hardly saw it happen, he leaped into the horse's saddle.

"Ladies and gentlemen of the cast," Jocko announced through his mike, "may I present to you Don Filipe of Spain and his famous dancing horse, Principe."

Tonia looked at Don Filipe, but Tiger had eyes only for Principe. Beautifully muscled, compact, standing sixteen hands high, the gelding had a coat of silver-white, dappled with black. His thick steel-gray mane and tail had been braided, and later unbraided, to fall in waves that fluttered with each movement. One ear forward, one ear back, wide eyes alert, the horse nickered softly and shook his head. Then he stretched out one front leg and arched his neck in a bow. As everyone applauded, Don Filipe smiled, showing dazzling white teeth.

39

Then Don Filipe looked annoyed, because he noticed that the young man who had brought the horse was still in the center of the stage, smiling a little as though some of the applause belonged to him.

"Ernesto! Out of the way, *tonto estúpido!*" Don Filipe barked. Ernesto threw Don Filipe an angry look before he turned and hurried into the shadows near the door.

"See, nobody likes to be yelled at in front of people," Tonia told Tiger, poking him with her elbow. "That Ernesto guy didn't like it one bit when that Don Filipe guy yelled at him. So you shouldn't think it's funny when Madame yells at Mom and Dad."

Tiger paid no attention to her. He was too enthralled with the horse. Wearing the same rapt expression he'd worn when he fastened himself to Chief the week before, Tiger crept toward the stage, toward the horse. He didn't even say goodbye to Tonia or Chief.

Tonia sighed. It happened all the time: Tiger went from one fascination to another. Whether it was a person or a hobby or an animal, when Tiger got hooked on something, he blocked out the rest of the world.

For a few weeks he would concentrate intently on whatever had caught his interest. He'd ask questions, study, learn everything possible to know about it until he'd wrung the subject dry. Then he'd get attracted by something else.

At the beginning of the past school year it had been stamp collecting. Then soccer, then a study of the earth's rock layers, or maybe it was model-ship building; Tonia couldn't remember which order they'd come

40

in. Two months ago he'd gone into scuba-diving with Heather—that had lasted longer than usual, probably because Heather was so good-looking. Last week it was Chief, which hadn't lasted very long at all, and now it looked as though it would be the horse Principe.

"Where did Tiger go?" Chief asked.

"To look at the horse." Maybe the old man would be lonely—Tiger hadn't left his side for a whole week, except when one or the other of them was onstage. "Don't worry, Chief. I'll stay here and keep you company," Tonia assured him. She looked up to see whether Chief appreciated her generous offer, but his face showed nothing.

"Take your places, boys and girls. We'll run through the whole number with the horse," Jocko announced.

Until that moment, Tonia hadn't known that a horse could really dance. But Principe could, in a way that sent shivers up the back of Tonia's neck. While the chorus kept to the background, and Mona and Casey and the other principals snapped their heels and their heads and swirled around him, Principe reared up to stand on his back legs. With his front hooves, he thrashed the air in a rhythm that seemed to match the dancers'. Responding to slight pressure from Don Filipe's legs, Principe broke into a piaffe—a trot in place. Then he did a slow pirouette, his muzzle missing by mere inches the ring of dancers. After the dancers faded backstage, Don Filipe guided the horse through a Spanish walk: moving in a tight circle, Principe extended one front leg after the other, straight out, in perfect time to the music. Again standing on his back

41

legs for what seemed an incredibly long time, Principe came down into a final bow.

With everyone else—dancers, singers, stage hands, electricians, the whole company—Tonia jumped up to applaud.

"Marvelous! Flawless!" Jocko and Ben cried as Don Filipe rode Principe into the wings.

"Flawless, my foot!" The angry shout came from Stan, the stage carpenter. "You want to see flaws—just come down here and look at what that horse's hooves did to my stage! This brand-new, gorgeous hardwood stage is full of dents from that big horse. From now on I'm going to put down a piece of masonite to protect the stage during the Spanish number."

"Masonite! Masonite!" Madame yelled, sounding anguished. "Oh no! You will not put down masonite for the flamenco dance. What sort of sound would my dancers' heels make on masonite? Hup tup tup—it would be nothing! *Nada!*"

"I don't care! They're not going to knock holes in my stage!" Stan hollered, but Madame was yelling even louder, "I insist that you leave the stage as it is. . . ."

Jocko held the mike right against his lips to bellow into it, "*Quiet!* Everyone take an hour break for lunch while we get this problem straightened out. Be back at two-thirty."

Tiger headed straight for the horse.

Four

At the beginning of the third week, Tiger got his big scene.

"We're going to start rehearsing the Gold Rush number," Jocko said into the mike. "Tiger, you're a newspaper boy. This is the scene: the chorus boys will be loafing inside a country feed store, and you come running in, waving a newspaper. Hold it up high so the audience can see the headlines. Big black letters will say 'Gold Discovered at Sutter's Mill.' So you—"

"Like this?" Tiger broke in before Jocko finished. "*Ex*-tra, *ex*-tra," he yelled. "Read all about the fabulous gold strike at Sutter's Mill in California. Want to buy a paper, mister?" Tiger ran from one chorus boy to another, thrusting a make-believe newspaper into each surprised face. "Here, mister, how about you? Want to read about the big gold strike? How about you, mister? Don't miss this exciting story about the discovery of gold in California. A real bonanza! Read all about it! This is the discovery of the century!"

"Uh . . . Tiger, I think you're overacting," Jocko

broke in. "You don't need to chew the scenery. You're supposed to be an ordinary newsboy, not Robert De Niro."

Chief tugged Tonia's arm. "How is it that your brother is talking so fast?" he asked.

"Fast? For Tiger, that's not so fast. He can talk a whole lot faster than that when he gets going."

Chief looked puzzled. "But I thought Tiger couldn't speak right. I thought something was wrong inside his head, or with his mouth. Always when he talks to me, he talks so slow."

Tonia squealed, "Oh no! Tiger was talking that way for your benefit, Chief, because he read somewhere that Indians don't like to be asked a lot of questions. Tiger's always full of questions—he can ask more questions than Trivial Pursuit. But he didn't want to offend you," she explained, "so he asked them real slowly. I told him that was bizarre. . . ."

"I would not have been offended," Chief said, looking offended. "I would not expect a white child to know the manners of my people. Especially only a little boy like Tiger."

"He's not so little," Tonia told Chief. "I mean, yes, he's little if you consider his size, but he's a lot older than he looks. He's twelve. Didn't he tell you how old he is?"

"I did not want to ask him," Chief replied. "To ask such questions is not polite."

Tonia clapped her hands over her mouth to stifle the laugh that wanted to come out. Chief smiled, then began to chuckle in a grating, breathy sound like a rusty

44

gate rasping back and forth. His mouth caved inward, almost disappearing inside a mass of laugh wrinkles. Tonia saw that Chief didn't have many teeth.

"Wait'll I tell Tiger," she began.

"Don't make him feel bad. He's a good boy. It's good for a boy to be curious, so he can learn things."

"What about a girl?" Tonia asked. "Is it good for a girl to want to know things?"

Chief considered. "I guess okay. What you want to know?"

Tonia settled herself more comfortably on the floor. She preferred floors to chairs.

"Well, I always heard that Indians could speak in sign language. Could you teach me some sign language?" she asked. "I mean, I got sort of interested in it because scuba divers use hand signals underwater— for danger, or distress, or just to communicate. Tiger's really into scuba right now, and he taught me a few signs. But Indian signs would be even better. So show me some. Okay?"

Solemnly, Chief raised his hand, palm facing Tonia. Then he waggled his wrinkled, crooked, knob-knuckled fingers up and down.

"What does that mean?" Tonia asked.

" 'Bye-bye.' "

"Huh?"

"It means 'goodbye. So long. I'm going away somewheres.' "

That time Tonia didn't attempt to hold back her laughter. Chief had made a funny joke! "It means 'goodbye' in white-people talk, too," she giggled. "You're just

45

faking me out, aren't you? Are you really an Indian?"

"Are you really a paleface?" he asked. His eyes crinkled in amused slits. "Yes, I teased you just then. I don't know sign language. Do you?"

"How about this?" Tonia crossed her arms in front of her chest, grasped her shoulders, and began to shake. "That means, 'Why do they keep this place so cold?' "

"How 'bout this?" Chief reached up to scratch his head with his long, bony fingers. "That means, 'I don't know.' "

"How about this?" Tonia pinched her nostrils together. "This means, 'Tiger's acting stinks.' "

Chief wagged his forefinger at her. "This means, 'You shouldn't be so hard on your nice brother.' "

Just then the chorus boys started to sing, which gave Tonia the chance to hide the little sting of hurt she felt. Here she was, trying to be nice to old Chief because her brother had deserted him, and Chief defended her gnarly little brother. Tonia was half tempted to desert Chief, too, but she hesitated. Where would she go?

Except for Tiger, Tonia was the only kid in the cast, so it got lonely. And boring. No one else in the cast wanted to hang around with her. She wouldn't expect them to, because they were all grown-ups. Chief was too old for them to pay attention to; Tonia was too young.

Somewhere, outside in the real world where the sun shone, Tonia's friends had fun together. They shrieked with excited laughter as they splashed down the watery coils of the Hydrotube. They crouched above water skis that sliced the surface of Lake Mead into ripples. Around blue swimming pools, Tonia's friends danced

46

to rock music while their skins turned glorious shades of tan.

In the dim WestAmerica Hotel showroom, Tonia's pale, pasty skin remained the color of a lizard's underside. The showroom's high ceiling echoed music that would appeal to middle-aged parents who could pay for tickets to the show, but not so much to their kids. The room seemed an enormous cage to Tonia, and she was a prisoner in the cage. A prisoner of love—that was the title of a song her mom sometimes sang. A prisoner because of guilt.

She'd always felt guilty about not being pretty, as though she'd let her parents down. Mona and Casey would have preferred a slender, graceful, beautiful daughter who looked like a porcelain ballerina, the kind that whirled on the tops of music boxes. Not that they'd ever let on to Tonia, but she knew it just the same.

Because she felt she was a disappointment to her parents, Tonia had agreed to do the show. To give her mother's dream a chance to come true, Tonia was willing to get up there and clomp around onstage, as much as she hated it. If she'd been pretty, and looked nice onstage, she might even have enjoyed it. That was possible.

She sighed, and dropped her chin onto her fists.

Chief said, "I know what that sign means. It means, 'I am sad.' "

Tonia grunted.

Chief patted her shoulder. She could feel the concern in his hand. "This sign means," he said, " 'I am sorry that you are sad. I will take your sadness into myself and help you carry it.' "

His kindness made her feel like crying. So she wouldn't break down and blubber, Tonia kept her blurry eyes straight ahead on the stage. The dancers were still learning their routine while the chorus boys sang:

"With a pick and a shovel and a . . . sack of dry beans,
I'm headin' out to Californ-eye-ay,
With my map and my grubstake in the . . . back of my jeans,
And a mule to keep me company a-long the way. . . ."

Tiger had disappeared from the stage. He was going to be in big trouble if Jocko decided to rehearse the number again from the beginning. Tonia knew where he was, of course—with that dumb horse. No, the horse wasn't dumb; the horse was smart. It was Tiger who was dumb, sneaking away during rehearsal. "Terribly unprofessional," Mona would say if she knew, and Casey would say a lot worse than that.

As the chorus boys neared the end of the song and dance, Tonia halfway held her breath, waiting to see what would happen. Would Jocko call the Gold Rush number again from the beginning? Part of her didn't want Tiger to get in trouble; part of her did. After all, Tonia was sitting there acting professional while Tiger goofed off.

. . .

Tiger was exactly where Tonia suspected: in the air-conditioned stable that had been built on the hotel parking lot. The air conditioning was one of the things that

48

made Ernesto furious. "In my country, people don't have enough to eat," he said. "In this country, horses get air conditioning. Pah!"

"I don't think very many horses in this country have air conditioning," Tiger tried to explain. "It's just that Las Vegas gets to be a hundred and ten degrees in the summer. Hotter than that, even. Over in the rich part of town, where Wayne Newton lives, some people build underground stables to keep their horses cool." Tiger stroked Principe's wavy mane, glad that Principe had a comfortable place to stay.

"What matters more?" Ernesto asked, his black eyebrows knotting into a scowl. "Horses, or people? The world starves, and *norteamericanos* spend money to keep horses cool. Or in this city, to make lights go blink, blink. The money it costs to light the Las Vegas Strip for one week—just one week!—could feed for a whole month all the people in my *población.*"

"In your pob . . . what?"

"*Población. Barrio.* Or, how you say it in American —slum."

"Oh." Tiger lowered his long lashes, feeling uncomfortable, even though he wasn't responsible for the air conditioning in Principe's stable, or for the lights on the Las Vegas Strip. "Población." He tested the word, trying to say it the way Ernesto did.

"Población." Hardly pronouncing the 'b,' Ernesto corrected him.

Before the población, Ernesto had lived in a village, but he was very small then, and he had a different name —Lalo. Then, too, he had a brother named Raul, who was a year younger. Both Lalo and Raul were too little to go to school, but their father went to school, because he was a teacher. Papa taught school until the day the dictator shot the president, and after that the government changed. Papa lost his job because he belonged to the wrong political party.

"Was it bad, living in the población?" Tiger asked.

"Sometimes good, sometimes bad. Mostly it was bad," answered Ernesto, formerly Lalo. The bad part was Papa trying to earn enough to feed them. Early in the mornings, Lalo went with Papa to the farmers' market, where they picked out the best avocados, the best peaches and bananas for Papa to sell on the street. But too often Papa couldn't work, because the *carabineros* came to take him away for questioning.

Principe arched his neck over the door of his stall and nipped Ernesto's shoulder, hard. "Stupid animal!" he shouted in a rage, as he whirled to punch the horse's muzzle, making Tiger cringe. "This horse hate the guts of me and I hate the guts of him."

Tiger felt in his shirt pocket for sugar cubes. Every time he and his parents and his sister ate in the West-America Hotel coffee shop, during rehearsal breaks, he took a few sugar cubes for Principe. He felt terrible that Ernesto had hit the horse, but at the same time, he felt sort of sorry for Ernesto. It was true that Principe didn't like Ernesto, yet the horse never nipped Tiger. His breath was soft and gentle on Tiger's hand as his lips daintily plucked the sugar.

"If you lived in a city slum, how'd you learn to take care of horses?" Tiger asked.

50

"I left the city and got a job on a ranch."

"Here? In the U.S.?"

"No. In my own country."

"What is your country?"

"You don't need to know." The little boy Tiger was a pest with so many questions, but Ernesto had no one else to talk to during the day, except for the horse, whom he hated. "It's in South America, that's all. Please don't ask me again the name of my country."

. . .

His country had never been good to Lalo. After the carabineros came and took Papa away for good, the family had hardly enough money to buy food.

His brother, Raul, earned a little by singing on buses. He had such a sweet voice, and he sang such sad songs, that the bus passengers gave him a *peso* or two out of pity.

"Someday I'm going to make it big as a singer," Raul told Lalo. "Every year I'll try out in the television contests, and I'll practice my songs until someday I win. Then I'll go to the *Estados Unidos* and be a star."

Raul had his songs, but Lalo had no skills at all, except to beg for pesos on the streets. When he was big enough, he left home and found a job on a ranch, where he mucked out stables and carried feed for the horses. Little by little he learned other things about horses: to groom them—to curry and brush their coats till they shone; to tack them up so the bridles and saddles fit properly; to comb out their manes and their tails. He liked horses then, and became very good with them. But

51

every time he asked for his pay, the rancher said, "Be patient, Lalo. I will pay you your whole year's wages on Independence Day, when we take the horses to the city for the big parade."

At last it was almost Independence Day. On the night before, September seventeenth, Lalo and the rancher loaded the horses into the truck. Then they drove to the city. Lalo was excited, because he would go see his mother and take her his whole year's wages. And he would see Raul, whom he loved most of anyone in the world. More than his mother, even.

The city was festive on the holiday eve. Fresh spring blossoms sweetened the air, and everywhere Lalo saw costumes, decorations, and dancing. He wondered if Raul and his friends were playing their music some-where for the celebration.

"Give me my wages," he said to the rancher. "I want to take the money to my mother and my brother."

"Do they live here in the city?" the rancher asked.

"Yes, in the población. In La Hormida."

"I will give you your wages tomorrow, after the pa-rade," the rancher said. He told himself that if he paid Lalo just then, the boy would not come back to prepare the horses for the parade.

Lalo grew angry. "Now!" he yelled. "I want the money tonight. I want to see my mother and my brother."

The rancher hit Lalo hard across the mouth, crying, "Don't speak in such a way to me, you little scum. I said I'll pay you tomorrow, so you can wait till then."

Rage had filled Lalo when the man hit him. For a

year he had worked for nothing except his food and a place to sleep. He had received not a single peso. Maybe tomorrow the rancher would not pay him, either. Who knew? He seized a pitchfork and beat the man over the head with the handle. When he fell unconscious, Lalo took all the man's money and ran away to his home in the población.

Raul was not home when he got there, but his mother was happy with the money. For a whole hour, she was happy. Then the carabineros came to drag Lalo away, and they took back the money he had stolen.

"Hey!" one of the carabineros said. "I know this place. I know this boy. He's the son of that political radical who used to live here. This may be more than a simple case of theft. This boy may be a radical, too, like his dead father was."

Lalo tried to protest, but they didn't listen to him. They took him to the National Center of Investigations to find out what he knew. He knew nothing political, but they didn't believe him. They tortured him; then they threw him into jail.

.   .   .

The door of the stable burst open, revealing bright light that startled Lalo. He threw up his arms to keep the torture light out of his eyes, but then he remembered. He was in Las Vegas, and his name was Ernesto.

The sunlight, reflected in waves off the hot parking lot, turned Tonia into a broad, accusing silhouette where she stood in the doorway. "Boy, are you ever in trouble, Tiger," she said. "Jocko called for everyone in the Gold Rush number, and you weren't there. Jocko's

53

mad, Mom's disgusted with you, Dad's ready to chew your head off. . . ."

"All right, all right, I'm coming. You don't need to say any more." Tiger felt rotten enough. Even though Ernesto never spoke many words, the man seemed to cast a dark, disturbing shadow all around him. It made Tiger feel worthless, as though he didn't deserve the amount of world he used up.

Since he was already miserable, Tiger would rather not hear his sister blabber about how everyone in the cast was mad at him, too. He turned to give Principe one last hug, needing a little warmth in order to face what was coming.

Five

They waited till they reached home before they let Tiger have it. With both parents sitting tight-lipped in the front seat of the car, and Tonia and Tiger in the back, the ride home was grim.

As soon as the front door slammed shut behind them, Mona started. "I was so humiliated!" she cried. "Everyone knows your father and I have been in show business half our lives. So they assume our children understand professional standards of behavior."

"Listen to your mother," Casey bellowed, although neither Tiger nor Tonia had said a word. "I'm going into the kitchen to start dinner because it's late, but I'll let you know what I think of you at the dinner table, young man!"

Tiger immediately lost his appetite.

Their meals had been much simpler since they'd begun rehearsing *The Way the West Began.* Before that, when Mona and Casey danced in other shows, Casey could cook all afternoon, serve a lavish early dinner, and be on his way to work, with Mona, by 6

P.M. Now that the family rehearsed all day for the new show, they didn't get home until six or seven in the evening. That gave Casey no time to fuss over medallions of veal or chicken divan, so he served steaks or chops and salad.

While she set the table, Mona had plenty to say about Tiger disappearing during rehearsal. Not realizing she was doing it, she plunked down the plates and silverware to the cadence of her scolding words.

"Utterly . . . (plunk) . . . unprofessional . . . (bang) . . . behavior . . . (thud). Any child of mine . . . (thump) . . . do such a thing . . ." (CRASH!) She'd slammed a teacup a little too hard. "Now see what you made me do!"

Then it was dinnertime—broiled lamb chops and spinach salad. Casey took over the lecture.

"Ben Bass gave you two kids parts in this show mainly as a favor to your mother and me," he said, wagging his fork, with a spinach leaf stuck to the tines, as though it were a battle flag. "This is not some two-bit program in your junior high school, you know. It's a many-million-dollar production. You kids had better start taking it seriously."

"Why are you yelling at me?" Tonia objected. "I was right where I was supposed to be."

"Aha!" Casey said, spearing his lambchop with a knife; drawing blood. "Don't think I haven't been watching you, young lady. I've seen you slip back there in the shadows with that old Indian, just to sneak out of your warm-up exercises."

"Don't you know you could hurt yourself that way,

Tonia?" Mona chimed in. "If you try to dance with cold muscles, you could pull a hamstring."

Tiger looked relieved that the heat was off him for a moment, but Casey hadn't forgotten him.

"This is the rule from now on," Casey said, returning to Tiger. "You are not to leave the showroom unless Jocko has announced that your part of the cast can take a break. If Jocko says you have an hour break, then you must set the alarm on your wristwatch and *be back on time!* That fancy scuba-diving watch I bought you for your birthday has a nice loud alarm, as I recall, so you will have no excuses. Now eat your dinner."

Tonia lifted her fork to poke at her chops. She didn't feel much like chewing on a hunk of some poor lamb, after she'd been chewed out herself by her parents. She glanced at Tiger, who was pale and scared, all scrunched down in his chair. He looked as though he were awaiting death by hanging. Now what's the matter with him, she wondered. Dad wasn't *that* hard on him.

After a moment Casey, too, noticed Tiger's excessively scared expression. Casey frowned. Tonia could see her father mentally start to rewind the tape of all the words he'd said to Tiger, searching for the ones that had caused him to look so wretched. Suddenly, Casey's eyes focused on Tiger's wrist. "Your watch!" he cried. "Tiger, where is your watch?"

Tiger slid down farther, until his chin touched the rim of his plate. "I gave it to Ernesto," he said in a small voice.

"You *what!*"

Tiger slithered down even farther. After a few seconds of awful silence that hovered in the room like the eye of a hurricane, Tiger began to reverse direction. His bottom slid backward in the chair until his face once again appeared above the table. "I felt sorry for Ernesto, Dad. When he was my age, he was so poor he lived in a slum."

"Do you know how much I paid for that watch?" Casey's voice had stopped being loud. It sounded strangled. "That waterproof, mineral-crystal, pressure-tested scuba-diving watch? It cost me two hundred and forty dollars!"

". . . and Ernesto's family was so poor that they hardly had anything to eat . . ." Tiger said through lips that trembled.

"So giving him your expensive watch is supposed to make up for Ernesto's unhappy childhood?" Casey's voice was recovering its volume.

"You can't solve the problems of the world, Tiger, by giving your watch away." That was from Mona.

"But Ernesto doesn't have a watch, Mom. Not even a Timex, so he never knows what time it is. Don Filipe only pays him forty dollars a week, and he has to buy food and clothes out of that."

"Nonsense!" Casey's fist hit the table with a bang, making the silverware jump. "I don't want you to hang around with Ernesto any more, because he's filling your head with crazy stories. In the United States of America, no one works for forty dollars a week. Maybe that's the way it is in Ernesto's country, but in our country, a man can change jobs and earn as much as he wants, if he's willing to work hard."

"That's not true." Perhaps because Tonia spoke quietly, everyone stopped yelling and turned toward her. "Chief told me that on the reservation where he lives, people are really poor, and they work hard. They opened a shop to sell the leather stuff they made, but the shop failed. Then they tried to raise chickens and tomatoes on a farm they have, but they couldn't make enough to pay off the mortgage, so that failed, too. They got so desperate they tried to open a house of ill repute. Places like that are legal in Nevada, but the feds wouldn't let them."

Mona gasped, "Tonia!"

"It's the truth, Mom. Indian reservations are under federal law, not state law."

Looking really angry, Mona said, "I won't permit that kind of talk at the dinner table. And if that old Indian has spoken about such nasty things to you, I don't want you to go near him ever again."

"Hey, wait a minute!" Tonia stood up, clutching the edge of the tablecloth, making wrinkles fan out between her fingers. "You're not being fair. Look, Mom and Dad, you made Tiger and me be in this show when neither of us wanted to. Neither of us. And we still don't."

That got to them. Both Mona and Casey stirred as though their chairs had become sticky.

"Now you're telling us we can't spend time with the only two people in the company who bother to talk to us," Tonia went on. "Do you think that's fair to us?"

"Well . . ." Casey and Mona glanced at one another uncertainly.

"Tonia's right," Tiger said, also rising to his feet. "We ought to talk this over and negotiate a compromise."

Negotiate a compromise. That phrase must have come from the time Tiger was crazy about Perry Mason books. Good old Tiger, Tonia thought. When it came right down to crunch, Tiger could be counted on.

"Here's what I propose," Tiger said. "I'll ask Ernesto to give me back my watch—he'll do it, don't worry. Then each time there's a rehearsal break, I'll set the alarm just like you said, Dad, so I'll always be back on time. Mom, I think you ought to let Tonia sit with Chief as long as she promises to do her warm-up exercises. After all, poor Tonia doesn't have a single other friend in the whole cast except old Chief."

"Yeah." Tonia might have added a tiny catch in her voice, but that would have been overacting.

As Mona began to look remorseful, Tiger sat down.

"Well, all right," Casey said slowly. "As long as you both stick to your promises, we'll let things stay the way they've been. I guess the rehearsals are pretty hard on you kids, keeping you away from your friends, especially during summer vacation."

Tonia fought to keep her face somber—her eyes wanted to light up, because she'd just learned a very important lesson. It didn't always have to be parents who made their kids feel guilty. The process was reversible. Guilt could be a two-way street.

She deliberately dropped her fork onto the floor. As she bent to pick it up, Tonia made a face at Tiger, a mouth-twisted, eye-rolling look that meant, "Whew! That was close!"

Tiger rubbed his mouth hard with his napkin to hide his grin.

. . .

"Ernesto?" Tiger peered around the door of the cool, dim stable. "Are you in here?"

"*Sí.* Come in and close the door."

He was sitting on the floor, his knees raised, his back against the wall. "So they let you come back to see me again? I thought your papa would say, 'Stay away from that *bandido* Ernesto.' I am pleased he let you come. It get lonely for me, with no one to talk to."

"I'm sorry," Tiger had to tell him, "but I can only stay a few minutes. I came here for a certain reason, and then I'm supposed to go right back. Hello, Principe." He held out the sugar cubes that had grown crumbly in his hand, loving the soft, moist nibbling of Principe's lips against his palm.

Ernesto sighed. "Well, a little bit of company is better than nothing. Sit down here beside me after you get through pampering that horse."

Tiger sat down. The wall felt warm behind his back. Intense outside heat radiated through double layers of aluminum to warm the inside wall of the stable, in spite of the air conditioning that kept the interior cool.

"What is the reason you came to see me," Ernesto asked, "since this is not a visit for the sake of friend-ship?"

"Oh, it's that, too," Tiger assured him. "It's just . . .

61

from now on, I can only come here during rehearsal breaks. And I have to get back right on time. So . . ." He hesitated, wishing he didn't have to say it. "I mean, since I have to be able to know what time it is. . . ."

"You want your watch back."

"It's not my idea," Tiger cried. "As far as I'm concerned you could keep it forever. Only . . ."

"Only your papa paid a lot of money for this watch." Ernesto began to unbuckle it. "And he don't like for you to give away something this expensive. Especially not to me. Right?"

"Right," Tiger agreed miserably.

"So here it is." He reached for Tiger's arm and buckled the watch around his wrist. Ernesto's body warmth remained inside the plastic watchband; Tiger could feel it circle his skin.

"Don't be so sad, Tigrito," Ernesto told him. "I been expecting this. We are still friends, no? We'll drink together, to cement our friendship."

"Drink?" Tiger wasn't sure about that.

"This can of Coca-Cola. I have only one; therefore we must share it. It is warm, but what matters warm cola among friends?" Ernesto pulled back the flip tab, and laughed as the Coke bubbled over the side of the can. He licked the spilled Coke, wiped the can against his pants, and handed it to Tiger. *"Salud!"* he said. "To friendship."

It really was too warm to taste good, but Tiger didn't care. He didn't care, either, that he was staying longer than the few minutes his father allowed him. Gratitude filled him, because Ernesto had returned the watch so graciously, without making Tiger feel like a nerd. Sitting beside Ernesto, their shoulders touching, backs leaning against the warm wall as their hands passed the can back and forth, Tiger experienced for the first time the feeling of camaraderie between grown men.

"This remind me of my tenth birthday," Ernesto said.

"It does? Why?"

"It's a long story, and I don't want your papa to get mad again."

"So what if he does?" Tiger said recklessly. "Go ahead and tell me the long story."

Ernesto smiled and sipped the drink. "Maybe I make it short. This is what happen: When I was a kid, we didn't have any money for birthday celebrations. On the day I became ten, my mama and papa seemed to have forgotten that it was my birthday. Neither of them even told me *Feliz Cumpleaños.* And my brother Raul was nowhere around, so all day I felt pretty bad." He handed the can back to Tiger, who drank.

"It got dark. Raul was not yet home. I told my parents to go to bed, that I would wait up for my brother. I sat down outside our shanty, leaning against the wall in the darkness, watching the fireflies, listening for my brother's footsteps. At last Raul came home."

"Where had he been?" Tiger asked.

"Singing on buses, as usual. But he stayed on the buses very late to earn extra pesos so he could buy me a present. He wanted to bring me a Coca-Cola, which was a . . . how you say . . . a luxury, for us. When he had enough pesos, he try to buy a bottle of Coke, but

63

he had forgot about the bottle deposit. So he didn't have enough money after all."

"Then what?" Tiger leaned forward, wanting the story to have a happy ending.

"For hours Raul walk the streets looking for an empty bottle to trade for deposit. You see, in my country, children fight over empty bottles, so it is hard to find one. But at last Raul did. He brought me the bottle of Coke for my birthday, and we sat in the dark and shared it, as you and I are sharing this drink now. It was the best birthday I ever had."

Tiger leaned back and closed his eyes. The story had ended happily.

"Tell me about your tenth birthday, Tigrito," Ernesto said.

Tiger moved uneasily against the wall. "Oh . . . ah . . . it was nothing special. Just a little party."

A little party. Thirty of his classmates, in the big recreation room of the condominium complex, seated around a two-foot-square cake decorated with rocket ships and ten tall candles. Balloons everywhere. After the cake and ice cream came Merlini the Magician, one of the specialty acts from the show Mona and Casey were in. Merlini made his beautiful blond assistant disappear, and when he opened the box she'd vanished into, a real, live tiger was there instead. Not a full-sized tiger; just a cub with a rhinestone collar and a silver chain, but still it was a spectacular trick. "A tiger—get it?" Mona and Casey had asked, beaming at their son. "A tiger came to our Tiger's birthday party."

Ernesto didn't ask any further questions about the

birthday, for which Tiger felt even more grateful. In the silence, Principe neighed and kicked the side of his stall to get attention. It sounded as loud as a cannon going off.

"Stop that, *busca pleitos,*" Ernesto yelled.

"What's that mean? Boos . . . ?"

"It mean troublemaker. That horse is nothing but a troublemaker."

The warmth, the nearness, the Coke they'd shared, gave Tiger the courage to say, "Maybe if you'd treat Principe nicer, he wouldn't give you so much trouble. I mean . . . like, when he nipped you that time I was here before, you hit him awful hard." It had bothered Tiger, because it showed a cruel side to Ernesto that he'd rather not know about. "Maybe if you didn't beat on him so much, he wouldn't bite you," Tiger added cautiously, not wanting to offend Ernesto.

"You don't know anything about horses," Ernesto answered. "That's how you train them. They do something bad, you hurt them. Just like a little kid—if he play with fire, or run into the street, you smack him hard. Then he won't do it again."

Tiger couldn't remember ever being smacked by his mother, or by his father. Not even once. Tonia had pounded on him plenty, though.

"Why worry about dumb animals?" Ernesto asked. "It's people you should worry about. When I was in prison, I got treated a lot worse than I ever treat that horse."

"You were in prison?" Tiger's eyes widened. "What for?"

65

"Because I steal some money to give to my mother."

Ernesto had stolen. He was a thief. But he was telling Tiger about it. Did telling the truth make him an honest thief? "Was it a lot of money?" Tiger asked.

"To the man I stole it from, it was nothing. But they threw me into prison just the same. And they tortured me."

"Tor . . . How . . . how did . . . ?"

"Tiger, you look so surprise. So distressed. How is it that you can know so little about the ways of the world?" Ernesto reached out to tousle Tiger's hair. "They made me lie down on a board. They tilted it to make my head lower than my feet. From a hose, they poured water on my face, so my mouth and nose got full of water. Then they held a wire with a live electric current against my mouth. The shock made me pass out. I was only seventeen, not man enough to handle that kind of pain."

Coke rose in Tiger's throat; he wanted to vomit. He wanted to weep. "All because you stole a little money?"

"No, because they thought I knew political secrets. They were wrong. But you must never tell this to anyone, Tiger. If anyone find out I have a prison record, I would be deported. And if they send me back to my country, they will not put me into jail. No. They will stand me in front of a firing squad, and shoot me dead."

With vehemence, Tiger said, "Do you think I'd ever tell anyone?"

"Of course not." Ernesto stared into his eyes and asked, "Did you think I would say all this to you if I

66

didn't trust you? I am trusting you with my life. Give me your hand on it."

Their hands met, not in a polite handshake, but in the clasped-fist handclench of fellow revolutionaries.

.　　.　　.

The sign game with Chief got to be more fun as another week of rehearsal went by. Mostly it was Tonia who made up the signs, and she started adding funny facial expressions to go with them. She loved to hear Chief laugh.

His eyes would squinch down into the teeniest slits, and his lips would almost disappear as they sank backward into the spaces where his teeth were missing. Then, from the cavern of his mouth, came the rusty-gate chuckles.

"See! You're making the sign for laughing," Tonia would say, pointing to Chief's arms, which clutched his skinny belly after she'd especially tickled his funny bone.

One day, just for fun, they began to make up a little act using their signs. "Stick 'em up," Tonia said, pointing her forefinger at Chief, thumb up. "Give me all your money."

Chief turned his shirt pocket inside out. "Got no money."

"Give me what you got, then," Tonia said, holding out her hand, palm up.

"You'll get this!" Chief shook his fist at her. Then he flexed his arms like a strong man showing off, but Chief's scrawny biceps couldn't even make his shirt-sleeves bulge.

67

Tonia threw up her hands in mock fright. "That guy's dangerous. I better get out of here." She pretended to thumb a ride, jerking her thumb frantically as pantomimed cars whizzed by. Finally she flapped her arms and said, "Can't get a ride, so I'll fly."

They thought they were hilarious, but Tiger, who'd been watching them, stayed gloomy. "You better do your warm-ups, Tonia," he said. "Mom's looking this way."

"Tiger, you're about as much fun as a worm in a pitcher of Kool-Aid," she told him, but she began to exercise anyway. With her hands behind her head, she bent from side to side.

Chief sat down, his amused look straightening out into seriousness as he regarded Tiger. "Something's troubling you," he said.

"Yeah, I guess so." Tiger hunched in dejection. "A lot of things have been bothering me lately. Chief, do you think the planet Earth is still a good place to live?"

"You planning to move someplace else?" Tonia asked. "If you are, I'll be glad to help you pack." Rotating her index finger in a circle next to her ear, she said to Chief, "This sign means, 'My brother is kind of bizarre.' "

Tiger ignored her. "I mean, there seems to be something wrong with the way things are on earth. Don't you think so, Chief? Some people have too much of everything, while other people have nothing."

Chief nodded. "Not like the olden times. In my grandfather's time, one tribe would steal another tribe's

68

horses. After a while, the other tribe would steal them back. So things stayed pretty much even."

Tiger tilted his head, not sure whether Chief was making fun of him.

"These days, things are not so even," Chief said.

Tiger decided that Chief was taking him seriously. "Yeah, like . . ." Tiger said, "do you know that the money it takes to light the Las Vegas Strip could feed millions of starving children?"

"All this land once belonged to my people." Chief waved a wide circle with both arms. "No one else wanted this land, because the white man thought it was worthless. But we knew how to live here. Mother Earth let us take from her what we needed. Now that's all changed. My people don't starve, but they don't have much, either." Chief's eyes clouded, and his mouth drooped with sadness.

"Tiger, why do you have to be such a bummer?" Tonia asked, stretching out her leg as though she were exercising, but giving Tiger a little kick in the ribs with her toes. "Chief and I were having a real good time before you started glumming around."

"You never worry at all about the world's serious injustices," Tiger lashed at her. "You're happy just as long as you get your Snickers bars."

He was saved from certain squashing because just at that moment, Jocko called out, "Boys onstage, girls onstage—you too, Tonia. We're going to do the first run-through of the barn dance number."

Tonia groaned. She'd hoped, prayed, and had finally begun to believe that she wouldn't have to dance in anything except the first number, the Indian one. Each week Jocko added a new number to be rehearsed, while the cast continued to practice the ones they'd already learned. Tonia hadn't been put into the flamenco dance or the Gold Rush dance, and she'd felt a cautious sense of relief. But too soon. Now Jocko was calling her to be in the barn dance number.

"Yuck!" she said under her breath, wanting to stamp her feet all the way up to the stage. She didn't, though, because Mona and Casey were watching her. They seemed pleased that Tonia would be in another number.

From front stage, while she waited for the rest of the dancers to take their positions, Tonia noticed Tiger and Chief deep in conversation. Wasn't that just like that little gnarl of a brother, she thought. Since he could no longer dash out for quick visits to Principe, because Casey was watching him all the time, Tiger had decided to be friends with Chief again. What hurt her most was that Chief probably preferred Tiger's company to hers, even though she'd spent the past two weeks being nice to the old man. Without thinking about where she was, Tonia made a horrible face at Tiger.

A wave of laughter lifted up from the showroom floor. It took Tonia a little while to realize that everyone was laughing at the awful face she'd made. Embarrassed, she rolled her eyes and scrunched her head down into her shoulders like a turtle. The laughter got even louder.

In the moment of silence after the laughter died down, Jocko asked over the mike, "Tonia, can you do that again?"

70

"Do what?" she asked, squinting against a spotlight that had just snapped on. It pointed right at her.

"Make those faces, the way you did a minute ago."

"Like this?" When Tonia repeated them, there was more laughter.

Although Jocko spoke softly to Ben Bass, the mike picked up their voices. "What have we here? A baby Streisand, maybe."

"Look at that face! More like a junior-grade Fanny Brice, I'd say," Ben replied.

A tingle of pleased excitement fluttered in Tonia's insides, in spite of her embarrassment.

". . . work out a few extra bits of business for her . . ." the mike picked up, and ". . . maybe a few comic bits in the first number, too."

Comedy! If only they'd let her do comedy, and not make her dance! She hated to dance, because people laughed at her in a different way when she danced, or so she thought. They laughed because she looked ridiculous with her fat jiggling up and down.

It was better when people laughed at the funny faces she made. Tonia controlled that—she pulled the strings of her facial muscles deliberately, to crack people up. In school she always clowned around for her friends. She'd learned early that a fat girl has two choices: she can spend her life hiding behind open locker doors, and slinking down the halls pressed between thinner classmates to conceal her width, or—she can act the clown. Tonia had chosen to clown.

It surprised her that the grown-ups in the cast would laugh at her clowning the way her classmates did, but she accepted it as a gift. She hardly had time to feel good about it, though, before Buzzy, the choreographer, started to walk her through the barn dance routine.

"You're the only girl on stage when the curtain opens," Buzzy told her. "All the boys are here, waiting for the other girls to arrive. While they wait, they dance with you, and you're just thrilled about it, Tonia, because you're only a kid and you get to dance with all these good-looking guys. So act thrilled."

Following Buzzy's instructions, the boy dancers galloped toward Tonia in two single files. First, one came from stage left and whirled her left to right, then the next dancer came from stage right and whirled her right to left. By the time all twelve of them had spun her around, Tonia could do the steps perfectly.

"That's excellent, Tonia," Jocko said from the back of the room.

She peered into the showroom to see if the rest of the cast was smirking at her. They didn't appear to be.

Then her heart lifted, because she noticed Chief. He had a big smile on his face, and he was giving her a sign. Thumbs up!

Six

Monday morning the O'Malleys arrived at the showroom, each carrying necessary items and other less necessary things to help pass the time. On the table they'd staked out as their own during the first week of rehearsals, they put Mona's knitting and thermos of hot soup; Tonia's sweater and leg warmers; Casey's magazines—*Sports Illustrated, Modern Parent,* and *Show Biz*; and Tiger's book, *America's Horses and Ponies.* Tiger planned to read it straight through, from Andalusian to Zebrorse, but he'd already cheated. Curiosity made him look up Zebrorse first, to find out what kind of creature had such a strange name. The answer was obvious—a cross between a zebra and a horse.

It was the beginning of the fifth week of rehearsals, and a few faint but encouraging signs indicated that a real show might emerge from all the chaos. Some of the dances were starting to look polished. A few of the problems had been solved: they'd found an acceptable Indian prayer for Chief; and Stan, the carpenter, had built a portable wooden floor to cover the stage when

Principe danced. That way the smooth new hardwood stage would be protected from Principe's hooves. Madame claimed that the sound of her dancers' heels wasn't as good on the portable floor as on the real stage, but what could one do? she asked. Shoulders raised, forehead furrowed, eyes lifted to heaven, Madame smiled ruefully and accepted the compromise.

The stagehands had begun to hang the flies, or backdrops, from pipes high above the stage. At the same time, the sets for the first number—the Indian number —arrived and were rolled into place. Costume designers had finished a few of the costumes, and were busy fitting them on the showgirls, but they fitted only six girls at a time so rehearsals wouldn't be disrupted. When a wardrobe lady put a tape measure around Tonia's middle, she closed her eyes and kept them closed until after the wardrobe lady made a mark in her book. Tonia didn't want to know the number of inches marked after her name.

That Monday morning, while Jocko drummed his fingers on the hand mike to make sure it was live, Ben Bass came to talk to the O'Malleys. "We've added several little bits of business to Tonia's two numbers," Ben said. "We think she's a natural as a comic. But we're concerned about a possible problem, and we want to keep it from going too far. It's about the way Tonia looks."

"Yes?" All the O'Malleys stopped what they were doing to stare at Ben.

"We don't want her to change the way she looks," Ben said.

Mona, Casey, Tiger, and especially Tonia were puzzled. "Change her looks?" Casey repeated. "How
would Tonia change the way she looks?"

"You know what I mean," Ben answered. "Tonia's
chubbiness. A lot of her comedy appeal is due to her
chubbiness. We don't want her to get too thin. She's
slimmed down quite a bit since rehearsals started."

"She has?" This time everyone turned to stare at
Tonia.

"I have?" Tonia squeaked.

Each day she put on a freshly laundered leotard and
tights, stretchy from the dryer. After a long day of
rehearsing, followed by a quick, lean dinner at home,
Tonia slid into her elastic bathing suit for an hour in the
pool, where she helped Tiger on and off with his scuba
gear, if Heather was gone. At bedtime she changed into
one of several long, loose T-shirts she slept in. She
hadn't worn jeans or a dress in weeks.

If she'd lost weight, she hadn't noticed. Everything
she wore either clung to her because it was stretchy, or
hung loose because it was intentionally sloppy. She had
noticed lately, though, that she could talk without
puffing while she did her warm-ups.

"I never thought that Tonia was particularly overweight to begin with," said Mona, proving that mothers
can be blind in their loyalty.

"We could always pad her costumes to make her look
fatter," Casey said.

Pad her costumes! Never would Tonia have believed
that people would want her to look fatter than she was.

"Tonia, here's five bucks from your old friend Ben

the producer," he said as he handed her a folded five-dollar bill. "Do me a favor and spend it on milkshakes." Ben winked at Casey. "Cheaper than padding the costumes," he said. "In fact, Tonia, you can go to the hotel coffee shop right now and order a milkshake. Order two if you want. For the next hour or so, we have to rehearse one of the specialty acts. Morton Pyke and his trained seals."

Tiger became immediately interested, but not because he cared anything about seals. "For the next hour or so?" he asked.

"Yes. We have to do their tech rehearsal today, and get their lighting figured out, because Morty and the seals leave tonight for Hollywood. They're appearing in a circus for the next few weeks, and they won't get back here until just before our show opens."

"Dad, may I . . . ?"

Casey frowned in his fatherly manner. "Yes, Tiger, you may go and see the horse for exactly one hour. Set the alarm on your watch. It's now 10:17, so be back here promptly at 11:17. Understand?"

"Yes sir, Dad! Absolutely. If I'm one minute later than 11:17, you can ground me for the rest of my life."

Ben laughed, but Casey didn't think it was funny.

.   .   .

Usually Ernesto exercised Principe very early in the morning, before the temperature rose above ninety, by walking him around the WestAmerica parking lot. Usually, by the time Tiger and his family arrived for rehearsals, Principe had long since finished his exercise walk and had been returned to his stall.

But early that Monday morning, Ernesto had smelled the storm. When he awakened at five-thirty, arising from the cot in Principe's stable where Don Filipe made him sleep, he went outside to check the dawn sky. Black clouds hung heavily to the west of Las Vegas. From the mountains in the west to the mountains in the east, clouds dappled the dawn with ridges. A mackerel sky, Ernesto's father had called it. Heavy rains would arrive in a few hours. The morning would be cool, and Ernesto could exercise Principe later, without worrying about the heat. He yawned and went back to bed.

Because Ernesto walked Principe so late that morning, Tiger got to take part in the exercise routine. He could hardly keep his feet from jiggling with excitement. For a while Tiger kept pace with the horse, walking next to Principe's shoulder. Then he darted ahead a few steps and ran back, using up energy as he tried to gather courage to ask if he could hold the lead shank. He couldn't find the right moment to break in and ask, because Ernesto wouldn't stop talking.

"How is it that so much money stays in the hands of so few? And why is it that all the power belongs to only three big nations, letting them force their will on the small countries?" Ernesto's questions could not be answered by a twelve-year-old boy, but Tiger was the only person who listened to them that morning. Other people entered or left the hotel, but they paid no attention to Ernesto, except to look with curiosity at the horse he led.

Tiger tried to make sense of Ernesto's questions, if only to answer "yes" and "no" in the right places, but his mind wasn't on world politics that morning. He wanted to hold that lead shank! Principe looked so beautiful, moving like the flow of quicksilver, his head rising and bending to the rhythm of his walk. When he tossed his head, his dark mane swept across his forehead like a child's bangs; to Tiger, Principe had all the best qualities of humans. Tiger loved it when Principe snuffled the back of his neck and blew warm breath against his skin, almost as if he wanted to tell Tiger they were friends.

"It used to make me sad. Now it makes me angry," Ernesto went on about the bad conditions in his homeland. "Maybe now is too late for the people in my country. I get despair about this, but then I think, maybe is not too late to show the rest of the world."

"Ernesto, would it be okay if I . . . ?" That was as far as Tiger got before a loud crash of thunder made Principe prance sideways in fright. The horse quivered and his nostrils flared wide.

"Don't be such a sissy, stupid horse," Ernesto said, yanking the lead rope. "Silly horse is always afraid of loud noises. Not me; I like loud noises."

Tiger's hopes sank. If the storm frightened Principe, Ernesto would never let Tiger lead him.

"You want to get attention, Tiger? Huh? Then make a big boom. Yeah. Not just horses pay attention when you make a big boom. Everyone notices a nice loud explosion." Ernesto laughed.

.   .   .

He knew how to make explosions. During all those months in prison, he'd learned.

So many times he'd tried to tell the carabineros that he wasn't political, that he wasn't a radical, but they hadn't believed him. They threw him into jail with a lot of real political radicals. Ernesto/Lalo learned from those men, who taught him how to plant bombs.

Only one week after he was released from prison, Ernesto/Lalo drove a car down Borgono Street and parked it in front of the National Center of Investigations. In the trunk of the car was a thirty-four-pound gelignite bomb.

An hour later, when the bomb exploded, Ernesto/Lalo was with his brother Raul, in a shack on the edge of the población.

Raul was very happy. "What good providence that you came home tonight, Lalo, and that you managed to find me. After Mother went to live with her sister in the south, I moved into this dump, but I'm leaving tomorrow. Leaving the country!"

"How can you leave?" Lalo asked. "Where did you get enough money?"

Raul laughed from the joy of telling it to Lalo. "I won the singing contest on television, just like I always told you I would. I got enough money from it to buy an airplane ticket to the United States. To Los Angeles. Look, I already have my passport and my visa," Raul said, pulling them from his shirt pocket. "See—there's my picture on the passport. I'm a handsome devil, no? Come on, admit it." He poked Lalo in the shoulder, the way he'd done since they were little boys.

"As soon as I make enough money, I'll send for you," Raul told Lalo. "You'll come to the United States and be my manager. We'll both get rich and famous." Raul laughed again, full of excitement over his good fortune. Lalo didn't have the heart to explain that he could never leave the country because he could never get a passport, now that he had a criminal record.

The noise began then—the squeal of jeep tires, the changing volume of heavy motors as truck gears roughly caught. The whine of motorcycles. Then the worst sound—the cough of machine guns.

The police were searching the población for someone. Maybe for Lalo. As they searched, they fired at random into the tumbledown shanties. People on the street screamed and ran.

Lalo dived to the dirt floor of the shack as bullets splattered through the flimsy walls. He was not hurt, but his brother Raul was shot. Instantly killed.

For only a moment could Lalo cradle his dead brother in his arms, because the carabineros would search every shanty, every lean-to in the población. With shaking hands he pulled the passport and the visa from Raul's shirt pocket, wiped the blood off them with Raul's handkerchief. He opened the passport to study the picture, which looked so much like him—Lalo and Raul had sometimes been mistaken for twins. He examined the name, Ernesto Raul Lagos. Raul had always gone by his middle name. Never by his first name—Ernesto.

.　　.　　.

The wind blew hard, bouncing candy wrappers and sheets of newspaper across the asphalt parking lot of the WestAmerica Hotel. On the horizon, black clouds had broken loose from the mountain peaks to roll ponderously toward Las Vegas. Another drum of thunder made Principe jump sideways and throw his head.

"Shouldn't we take him inside his stable?" Tiger asked Ernesto. "That looks like it could turn into a really huge storm, and Principe acts scared already."

"The horse is so pampered—it won't hurt him if he get a few raindrops on his rear end," Ernesto answered.

"I don't think it's going to be only a few raindrops," Tiger said. "This could be one of those flash-flood storms that hits Las Vegas about every year. You know, if only half an inch of rain falls on those mountains over there, by the time all the water runs down here to the city, it can get four feet deep in the streets."

"You have seen such a thing happen?"

"Sure. Once Caesar's Palace parking lot got flooded so bad that the cars floated around like toy boats. If I'd had some scuba gear, I could have been the first person ever to go scuba diving in a parking lot."

"You know how to scuba dive?" Ernesto asked.

"Yeah."

"You are good at it?"

"Well, let's say that for my size, I'm the best scuba diver in the entire state of Nevada." It was a painful joke that Tiger made. All the other people his size happened to be eight or nine year old kids, too young to deep-water dive.

Ernesto seemed impressed. "The best in the entire state of Nevada? Truly?"

"For my size, I said." Tiger had the words ready to

81

explain, but an angry yell stopped him as Principe nipped Ernesto from behind.

"Animal torpe! Caballo odioso!" Ernesto shouted. He yanked the lead shank to force down Principe's head. Then, with a swift motion, he twisted the horse's ear viciously.

Principe screamed and jerked his head. The force of the movement broke the snap that attached the lead shank to his halter. Fear and pain made the horse's eyes widen, showing white rims. Ears flat, he reared and lunged with a gaping mouth toward Ernesto, but Ernesto dashed out of the way of those dangerous teeth.

At that moment, Principe realized that nothing restrained him—no lead shank, no rider, no gate or fence. For a few seconds, as confusion showed in his rolling eyes and wavering ears, he pranced from side to side. Another peal of thunder, much louder than the ones before, crashed overhead.

The veins in Principe's head stood out. His muscles contracted, then exploded to carry him in a great surging leap that ended behind a blue Volkswagen just backing it out of a parking space.

The startled driver hit his brakes and horn at the same time, frightening Principe even more. He began to gallop around the parking lot, his hooves striking sparks on the concrete while lightning shot sparks a million times more powerful through the darkening skies. Tiger and Ernesto ran after him, yelling and trying to head him off, but Principe paid them no attention. He galloped between rows of cars, unable to see the low red Z car that rolled slowly along the end of one lane.

Its driver craned his head sideways as he tried to find a place to park, never suspecting that a half-ton horse raced toward him. Just as Principe reached the end of the rows of cars, the Z car driver gunned his motor—he'd seen a space, and he wanted to get it before another driver did. The red Z car shot forward so fast that Principe couldn't stop in time.

Ernesto shouted, Tiger covered his eyes, and Principe sailed into the air like Pegasus, folding his front legs tightly underneath his chest, stretching his hind legs out behind in the manner of an eagle in flight. He soared over the Z car without chipping off even a flake of its red paint.

Principe landed hard on his front feet, but didn't stumble. Picking up speed as he landed, he galloped away as the driver of the Z car, a portly middle-aged man wearing lemon-yellow tennis shorts, climbed out of his car, looking terrified.

"You go that way, I go this way," Ernesto yelled to Tiger.

The rain began to fall then, in torrents. Since Principe was a horse with enough sense to come in out of the rain, he headed toward the large door through which the stage sets had been carried inside by the crew. It was fortunate the huge roll-up door stood open, because Principe never slowed from his gallop.

"Catch him! Catch him!" Ernesto bawled, but that was impossible to do. No matter how fast they ran, they were no match for Principe's speed.

When they got backstage, the place was in a wild uproar. Principe had kicked over a tub containing fish that were fed to the seals to reward them when they performed. Two of Morton Pyke's famous seals clapped their flippers and barked wildly, while two others slithered around the stage gobbling as many fish as they could grab. Morton Pike himself sat flat on the stage, having slipped on a fish and taken a pratfall.

Stan, the carpenter, jumped back and forth yelling, "My stage! Look what's happening to my beautiful stage! Look at those gouges! Look at this mess!"

As Don Filipe tried to calm him, Principe stood trembling, his ears moving and his eyes white-rimmed. Several of the showgirls still shook in their fright over seeing a horse run wild around the stage. Hollering into hand mikes, Jocko and Ben were hurrying forward from the back of the showroom. In the midst of all the confusion, just at the moment Ernesto reached Principe, Don Filipe unleashed a punch that knocked Ernesto to his knees.

"Viejo desgraciado!" While he shouted a stream of furious Spanish, Don Filipe began to beat Ernesto with a thin, short horsewhip. Two of the chorus boys rushed to hold Don Filipe's arms, but he continued to scream his rage. "First you will clean up this mess, and immediately after that I will have you deported to your own wretched country."

"No, Don Filipe, no!" Ernesto appealed to him, kneeling on the floor among the slithery fish and the greedy seals. "Don't have me deported. Please, *señor,* I beg you to forget this unfortunate mishap." He tried to pick up the fish, but he reached for too many at once, and they spurted from his arms.

84

How he hated the smell of fish, and the smell of the ocean! To Ernesto it was the smell of death. The night Raul died, Ernesto had escaped the police search, running through the dim alleys of the población with the sound of dogs and boot-shod feet sometimes so close that he had to hide in doorways.

With Raul's passport and visa clutched tightly against his chest, Ernesto had run to the only place he could think of—the farmers' market. At three o'clock in the morning, the farmers' market was filled with activity, with people from the countryside bringing in their fruits and vegetables to arrange for sale to dealers at dawn.

A drunken truck driver was trying to unload fish into the stalls, but the fish kept slithering out of his hands as though they were alive.

Ernesto heard sirens, and saw carabineros patrolling the streets with their guns drawn, so he ran to help the fish man, pretending he belonged on that job.

"It is kind, young stranger, that you do this for me," the fish man said. "I think I had bad wine at supper."

"I think you had too much wine," Ernesto told the man.

"What is your name?" the man asked him.

He almost answered "Lalo," but he caught himself in time. "Ernesto."

"Very well, Ernesto, you wish to make some pesos? You know how to drive? When we get all the fish out of the truck, you drive me home while I sleep off this bad wine. You want to do that?"

"Where is your home?"

"In the big city on the ocean shore. At———." The man named a famous resort a few hours' drive away.

A seaport town. From there Ernesto could find a ship to take him out of the country, this country that killed fathers and brothers, and tortured people. "I will drive you," he said. It was fortunate he'd learned to drive when he worked on the ranch.

By the time they reached the ocean resort, the fish man had sobered and was in a bad mood. He gave only ten pesos to Lalo. Not Lalo—Ernesto. He had to start thinking of himself as Ernesto because of the name on the passport.

In the resort town, near the huge white casino, Ernesto noticed a poster on a wall. It advertised Don Filipe and his dancing horse, Principe, who were performing in the South American resort town for two weeks.

Ernesto learned where Principe was stabled, and hung around the place, trying to make friends with the stableboy, named Luis.

"How much does he pay you, this Don Filipe?" Ernesto asked Luis. "Whatever he pays, I'll do all the work for a third, and you can keep the rest of the money." When Luis didn't answer, Ernesto said, "For a fourth. I'll do all the work for only a fourth of the money."

"A fifth," said Luis. Ernesto agreed.

He slept on the floor outside Principe's stall, covering himself with straw. After a few days, Don Filipe began to recognize Ernesto, and sometimes sent him on errands for a few pesos.

Then it came time for Don Filipe and Principe to go to the United States to perform. The stableboy Luis would go with them. They would travel by steamship, because it was difficult to arrange air transportation for Principe.

When the ship was about to leave, Don Filipe paced the deck, scowling, waiting for Luis to show up. Instead, Ernesto raced up the gangplank. "Luis refuses to come," Ernesto told Don Filipe. "He says he has fallen in love with a waitress from the casino, and he cannot bring himself to leave her."

(Luis could not bring himself to leave the resort because his hands and feet were tied together, his mouth had been taped shut, and he was locked inside the tack shed next to the stable. He lay dazed and bleeding from the beating Ernesto had given him.)

Hoping, anxious, Ernesto added, "Luis says that I can have his job, since I am so good with the horse."

"Luis says that, does he?" Don Filipe stormed. He was furious, but in only minutes the ship would leave the dock, and he needed a stableboy. "Do you have travel papers?" he snarled at Ernesto.

"I do, señor." Ernesto produced his brother's passport and visa. "See—this is me. Ernesto Raul Lagos." Hardly breathing, he waited for Don Filipe to examine the picture on the passport.

"Get that thing away from my face!" Don Filipe knocked the passport from Ernesto's hand. "All right,

87

I'll take you along, but you won't receive one cent of wages until your steamship ticket has been paid back in full. Agreed?"

Ernesto agreed. He would have agreed to anything to get away from that country before the carabineros caught up with him.

He had never traveled over water before, not even in a rowboat. During the whole week of the voyage, Ernesto was miserably sick. Each chance he got, he hung over the railing to gulp air, staring at the blue-green waters that roiled beneath him. The ocean frightened him. A man could die underneath all those different-colored layers of water. Sometimes he felt so sick he thought it wouldn't be such a bad thing to die. And one time, looking down into the water, he thought he saw the face of his dead brother Raul.

Or maybe it was his own face that he saw, beneath the surface of the waves.

.   .   .

Ernesto heard a strange beeping that repeated itself again and again. He became aware that Tiger was on his hands and knees beside him, helping to clean up the mess of spilled water and fish. The beeping came from the alarm on Tiger's watch.

"I can't turn it off. It has to beep ten times, then it quits," Tiger said, slightly apologetic about the watch, but very much worried about Ernesto. "Do you think he'll really have you deported?" he whispered. "Look, I got all the fish picked up."

Ernesto answered, "I never know for sure. But I think he will not. He threatens it every time he get angry with me. If he sent me away, who else would work for so cheap? Who else could he beat with his little whip to get his jollies?"

When Tiger looked even more distressed, Ernesto said, "Don't worry, *amigo*. Don Filipe is no more troubling to me than a mosquito. I have survived attacks by vultures."

Seven

The moment of truth had arrived for Buzzy, the choreographer. Every spark of his considerable talent had been used to create a dazzling finale for *The Way the West Began*. The finale didn't look at all Western, not in the cowboy-and-Indian sense; it was pure Las Vegas. Statuesque, long-legged showgirls, wearing feathers and sparkling beads on glittery fabric, descended a mirrored stairway to center stage. From both sides of the stage, male dancers and singers sang show tunes in praise of female beauty. Audiences expected that kind of spectacular ending to a Las Vegas show, and would have felt cheated without it.

That day, for the first time, the showgirls wore full costume for a run-through of the finale. Three-foot-high headdresses made of pheasant and ostrich plumes towered above their heads. Each headdress weighed fifteen pounds or more. They wore backpieces, too, that weighed twenty-five pounds and were made of feathers, carefully dyed and individually sewn in place to wave

90

gracefully when the girls moved. Each single costume had cost five thousand dollars to make.

That's why Buzzy gnawed his knuckles. If the girls couldn't manage the dance steps because their costumes were too heavy or awkward, Buzzy would have to change the dance. The costumes couldn't be altered— too much money had been invested in them. "Oh please," Buzzy muttered in prayer, "let the dance work. After all the blood I sweated over it, let it work!"

Tonia and Tiger sat in their usual places next to Chief. Tonia was enthralled by the wonderful way the feathers stirred as the showgirls swooped and glided, making them look like bright tropical birds in a land of fantasy. Tiger sat sunken in gloom.

As Mona appeared, all alone, at the top of the stairs, Tonia inhaled sharply and held her breath. From Mona's shoulders hung a royal-blue cape. Although the cape was extremely heavy, Mona moved like a queen, bending one shapely leg after another in perfect rhythm to descend the eighteen-step mirrored stairway. As she swept downward, the blue cape spread out behind her until it covered the entire width of the staircase, revealing, on the royal-blue velvet, the pattern of a peacock's tail. The effect was so exquisite, and her mother looked so beautiful, that Tonia felt close to weeping with pride and love.

"Six feet tall," Tiger said gloomily. "Look at them. Each of those girls is nearly six feet tall. It isn't right for that much height to be wasted on girls when I'm so short."

Angry because he'd spoiled the mood, Tonia huffed, "Well, if it isn't Mister Cheerful Slimeheart himself. Who cares if you're short? Anyway, everyone always makes a big fuss over you because you're so little and cute. If you had any sense, you'd be glad you're not tall."

"I get awful tired looking up at grown-ups chins," Tiger said. "I get tired seeing the hair inside their noses."

Chief shook with silent laughter and placed his fingers over his lips. That sign meant he was amused, but he didn't want to hurt Tiger's feelings by laughing out loud.

"The trouble is, I don't think I'm ever going to grow tall, no matter what Mom says about puberty."

"It doesn't matter," Tonia answered. "When you grow up, you don't have to be in shows like this where it's better to be tall. You can be in the movies, instead. There are lots of short actors in the movies. Look at Dustin Hoffman."

"Who says I have to be in show business?" Tiger yelled. "I don't want to! There are lots of other things I can be. A marine biologist. Or a geologist. I can be a lawyer. I can be president, for crud's sake. Maybe I'll turn out to be the shortest president in the history of the United States! That's *real* fame!"

"Yeah, what am I talking about?" Tonia muttered. "There *is* life outside show business." She made a face at Tiger. "But you didn't have to yell at me. And anyway, I know what's really bothering you."

Her smug look added aggravation to Tiger's gloom.

He would have liked to punch her, but he couldn't afford to get into additional trouble.

"You're just fizzed off because Dad won't let you go outside with the horse anymore," Tonia told him. "Not after that thrash-blaster stunt you pulled last week on the day of the big storm." She lowered her voice to imitate a TV weatherman. "Last week, the city of Las Vegas got dumped on by a furious cloudburst, and cute little Tiger O'Malley got dumped on by his furious father."

"Watch it, lizard lips," Tiger snarled. He really might have hit her then, but Jocko called loudly over the microphone, "Chief, where are you? Oh, I see you. Would you come onstage please?"

Chief quickly shook a finger at Tonia and Tiger, warning them to behave because he had to leave and couldn't referee their quarrel. As he made his way to the stage, Tonia forgot Tiger and his rotten mood to worry about how frail Chief looked. A man that old shouldn't have to spend long hours sitting around at rehearsals. He'd taken the job in the show, he'd told her, only so he could earn money to help his people on the reservation.

"Have you learned your lines, Chief?" Ben Bass always spoke respectfully to Chief. "That's good. Wardrobe people, where's Chief's headdress?"

They carried it out and placed it on his head, a huge warbonnet of eagle feathers. It could have been from a museum, Tonia thought—it seemed so real. Feathers on showgirls and feathers on an Indian; how different they looked. Feathers made the showgirls

93

glamorous, but they made Chief solemn and dignified.

"Lift your arms toward the sky, Chief," Jocko instructed him. "Now say your lines."

He was a frail old man with withered upraised arms, but when he spoke, powerful magic filled the room. Chief's words swelled up to where the backdrops now hung on the fifty-two overhead pipes. They swirled outward into the showroom, swept across tables that would soon seat twelve hundred paying guests, and brought tears to the eyes of more than one member of the cast. In a slow voice, too full for his bent body to rightly own, Chief said:

> "They are gone.
> The great herds,
> the hunters,
> the ghost dancers.
> All gone.
>
> Only worn shapes are left,
> Carved into rock.
>
> As long as rock lasts,
> As long as earth turns,
> Men and sheep will dance,
> Carved in the rock.
>
> But the men of blood,
> And the beasts of flesh,
> All are gone.
>
> Nono'si tugu'bi."

He bowed his head, as though he too would sink into the earth and disappear.

Tonia choked up.

She didn't understand what was the matter with her lately. Every day, it seemed, some part of the show got her all emotional. The constant rehearsing was doing it to her, she suspected—making her weepy all the time. Confined in the dim showroom hour after hour, watching the same people doing the same numbers over and over again as they tried to make them perfect, Tonia had begun to feel that the rest of the world didn't much matter. If it even existed.

When Chief returned to his chair, she put her arms around him and hugged him, not saying a word. He patted her shoulder. Neither of them noticed the figure that came toward them out of the dark shadows, but Tiger did.

"Ernesto! I'm so glad to see you. How's Principe?" Tiger fumbled in the pockets of his jeans and his shirt, so eager that his hands shook. "I have lots of sugar cubes—I've been saving them, 'cause Dad won't let me go outside anymore. Will you give them to Principe for me? Does he miss me?"

Ernesto paid no attention to Tiger. It was Chief he spoke to.

"I heard what you say on the stage," he told Chief. "Words are easy. But no one pays attention to words, old man. To make a difference in the way things are in the world, action is necessary."

Chief tilted his head, unsure of what Ernesto was talking about.

"Send these children away," Ernesto said, speaking softly. "I have something to talk to you."

Chief's fingers dug into Tonia's arm; she knew that he didn't want to be left with Ernesto. "What you have to say, you can say in front of Tiger and Tonia. These children are my friends. They are like grandchildren to me."

"Like grandchildren! Pah!" Scornful, Ernesto asked, "Do your real grandchildren own two-hundred-dollar wristwatches? Do they have nice blue swimming pools beside the poor shacks they live in? Tell me about your real grandchildren."

Chief lowered his eyes before he answered. His lips grew stiff as he said, "I have no descendants out of my own body. Once I had sons and daughters, but I have none anymore."

"And why is that, old man?"

Chief kept his eyes lowered. By raising them, he might reveal his dislike of the hostile young man who crouched before him, and that would be impolite. "If you feel that you must know, these are the reasons," Chief said. "The daughters died young of tuberculosis. One son was gored by a bull in a rodeo. Another son died of drink. Two sons got killed in war—one at Anzio, one on a beach in Okinawa. I never learned where those places are." Chief's spiderweb eyelids fluttered over the hurt in his eyes. "It is unnatural for a man to live longer than his children."

Ernesto leaned closer to Chief. "Do the children of the rich die of lung sickness? Did anyone bring medicine when your daughters lay sick? The son who died of drink—did he get drunk from despair?"

Tonia frowned, not liking what Ernesto said, but her

96

brother leaned forward. Tiger's lips opened partway in rapt attention.

"I inquire of people about certain things," Ernesto continued. "The light technicians—I talk to them." He waited for Chief to show interest, but when Chief remained silent, Ernesto went on.

"Those men, they tell me that a million and a half watts of electrical power will be used to light this show. Do you know how much that will cost? And just the computer console to work the lights is worth a quarter of a million dollars. What could your people on the reservation do with that much money? *Anda! Dimelo!* Tell me, old man!"

"Leave him alone!" Tonia said, but Ernesto gave her such an angry look that she pulled back. As Ernesto's dark young eyes glittered fiercely, Chief's dark old eyes grew dull with doubt.

"My head hangs in sorrow because my people are so poor," Chief answered. "My people came from the earth. The earth was our provider."

With his mouth close to Chief's ear, Ernesto said, "Someone stole your land, your earth. Someone stole your water."

"That I could never understand," Chief said. "Water, too, comes from Mother Earth, and belongs to all. Yet the white man believes he can own water. How can a man own water?"

"They stole it from you. They built that big dam to store the water that belongs to your people." Ernesto's voice was low, and so persuasive that even Tonia half believed him. "And what do they do with your water

97

that they stole? They turn it into electricity to light this decadent city."

When Chief frowned, Ernesto moved even closer to him. Both of them seemed to have forgotten Tonia and Tiger.

"Do you know what I can do? I can make all the lights of Las Vegas go dark."

The skin on Chief's hands looked like wrinkled brown wrapping paper, the shiny kind used in butcher shops. Tonia noticed Chief's hands because they'd begun to tremble.

"Why would you do such a thing?" Chief asked.

"To make a political statement. Do you think they would listen to any other kind of statement? You must join me in this, old man. For the sake of your people. You too must make a statement, about their poverty and suffering."

As Chief raised his troubled eyes and spoke, his voice began to tremble, too. "My people say that if a man has lived many days, he must know many things," he said. "But the world changes too fast. I think that I don't know enough. I don't know what could be done to help my people."

"Trust me," Ernesto said. Turning suddenly, he spoke to Tiger for the first time. "You also, Tiger. You as well must trust me."

Tiger nodded, and moved toward Ernesto. The boy and the two men drew together like conspirators; three heads almost touching—blond, black, and gray. The bottom edge of Ernesto's teeth showed white; he allowed himself the smallest smile of triumph because he

98

could so easily manipulate the boy and the old man. Even the girl, who sat just outside the triangle of males, leaned forward as though intrigued.

Whatever that smarmy Ernesto was up to, if anything, Tonia was determined to worm her way into it, even though he frightened her a little because he looked so scary and intense. Someone with sense had to be around to take care of Chief, and the only sane, sensible person seemed to be Tonia.

Actually, she thought Ernesto was nothing but a bizarre creep who talked crazy talk. Probably he just wanted people to notice him. Or maybe hanging around the fringes of show business, with all its make-believe, had pushed him over the brink into fantasy land. Tonia could understand that—the show was certainly having an unsettling effect on her.

She had to remind herself that she was in the show only for her mother's sake. Once she'd fulfilled Mona's dream, Tonia could live her own life far away from anything theatrical. The farther the better.

Eight

Casey had fallen asleep with the Sunday paper tented over his chest. He slouched on the sectional sofa, his long, tanned legs straight in front of him, his bare heels nested in the thick-piled carpet.

Tiger glumly studied his sleeping father. Casey wore a knit shirt with a little polo pony symbol on it. "Patagonia" was stitched on his shorts. The slim watch that encircled his wrist was real gold, and his golden hair had been carefully cut into a style perfect for his features.

The drapes on the window behind Casey had cost more than he and Mona wanted to pay for them, but they'd decided to "go for quality"—their words. Through the window Tiger clearly saw the Sunrise Mountains, a view that had added ten thousand dollars to the price of their condo.

If he turned so that his back was toward the view, Tiger could look into the solarium, a glass-walled room in the middle of the floor. The solarium had no roof, allowing a tree in the middle of it to grow straight up through where the roof would have been. That opening raised their air-conditioning bill quite a bit, but Mona and Casey believed the greenery was worth it.

Casey woke up when the newspaper slid off his chest and hit the floor. "Guess I dozed off," he said. "Are Mom and Tonia back yet?"

"No." They'd gone to buy Tonia some smaller jeans. "What's up, Tiger? What are you doing?"

"Nothing. Just thinking."

Casey yawned and stretched. "Want to share your thoughts with your old man?"

Yes, Tiger wanted to. He'd been waiting for the chance. "Why do we have so much when most of the world is starving?" he asked.

"Whoo!" Casey sat up straight. "That's a tough question to hit me with when I just woke up."

"Well, it bothers me, Dad. Do you know there's an Indian reservation right here in Las Vegas, in the city limits? Not Chief's reservation, but another one, even poorer. Here we are with all this expensive stuff, and just a few miles away, people hardly have anything."

Casey stretched out on the sofa, arranging his legs comfortably. "Things are like that all over the world, Tiger. Not just around here."

"Yeah, but Dad, before people like us came, the Indians had a good life on this land. They had enough to eat, and everyone was happy. Why didn't we just leave them alone?" Tiger slumped on an ottoman, his elbows on his knees, his eyes troubled. "Why did we have to ruin things for them?"

Casey answered, "We didn't ruin things, son. We

101

improved things. For the Indians and for everyone else. When the population of this country kept getting bigger, people needed more space, so they moved out here. And we fixed things so people can live in this climate. You can't hold back progress."

"Progress!" Tiger jumped up. "You call it progress to fill this city with electric lights that cost a fortune to turn on? Just so rich people can run around casinos playing slot machines and looking at shows? Ha! Some progress!"

"Hey! Wait a minute, Tiger," Casey said, beginning to get annoyed. "You're talking about things you don't understand. Some cities live on manufacturing, like Detroit. Other places turn out technology, like Silicon Valley. Las Vegas happens to make its living by providing entertainment. There's nothing wrong with that. And it's not just rich people who come here for entertainment—it's mostly the ordinary, everyday kind of people who come."

"Well, I think it sucks."

"Tiger!" Casey lunged to his feet, really angry. "Don't go smartin' off at me like that, buddy, or you'll get grounded forever. Listen, I'm not ashamed of what I do for a living. I'm a dancer, and a darn good one." Casey ran his fingers through his hair as though to calm himself. Then he walked around the coffee table to stand right in front of Tiger. He placed his hand heavily on Tiger's shoulder.

"Son, I don't have to justify myself to you," he said. "But your ideas are getting pretty screwed up lately, and I want to set you straight. What I do for a living is important, and not just to me. So pay attention to what I explain to you." He squeezed Tiger's shoulder hard, to turn on his attention.

"Suppose there's a couple," Casey said, "maybe from —Buffalo, New York. They save their money all year long to bring the family here to Las Vegas for a vacation. Now, I get up there on the stage and I give everything I've got—everything!—to please that audience out front. So when they go back to Buffalo, and they're paying their bills or eating a burnt dinner or shoveling snow that's up to their earballs, they can think back to the great show they saw in Las Vegas. And they'll feel good, remembering. People need what I give them, Tiger."

His voice low, his eyes lowered, Tiger said, "People need food a lot more. And clothes, and medicine when they're sick."

"Dammit, Tiger, I'm not God," Casey shouted. "I do the best I can. I give to United Fund. I give to African famine relief. If some poor schmuck comes up to me on the street and says he's hungry, I give him a couple of bucks. But I can't solve the problems of the whole world."

"Someone has to," Tiger answered.

"Well, good! You grow up and save the world, if you're so blasted smart."

"I will. Or at least I'm going to try to." Tiger lifted his head in defiance, but his lower lip trembled.

"Something tells me you've been talking to that Ernesto again," Casey said, his anger turning grim. "I thought I told you to stay away from him. You disobeyed me."

For a moment, Tiger didn't respond. He could have said that he never went near the stable, that Ernesto had been coming into the showroom lately, but he didn't want to get Ernesto into trouble. Meeting his father's eyes, Tiger said only, "I never once disobeyed you, Dad. Never."

Casey's tight lips relaxed. He breathed deeply, then muttered, "Aw, I knew that all along, kid. I'm sorry I said that. It's just—you're asking questions I don't know the answers to." He pulled Tiger close, holding the boy's head against his chest and mussing his hair. "I'm just an ordinary man, Tiger. I do the best I can to fill up my own little space in the world, and to provide for you and your mom and sister."

Tiger wasn't sure that was enough. He pulled away.

Casey had taken his wallet out of the back pocket of his shorts and was lifting money from the bill compartment. "Here," he said, holding out a ten and a twenty. "Take this and buy Ernesto a watch. You ought to be able to get a decent-looking Timex for this much. I still don't want you to hang around Ernesto, but you can give him a watch."

Tiger shook his head. "It's too late. Ernesto already has a watch. A nice one."

"See, I told you he has to be earning more than forty dollars a week," Casey said, looking smug because he'd won at least that much of the argument.

104

But Tiger was still shaking his head. "No, I don't think he is."

"Then how could he afford a nice watch?"

"I don't know, Dad. I don't know how or where Ernesto got it."

.   .   .

"You been circling around and around like a badger sniffing porcupine," Chief told Ernesto. "Come out and say what it is you're sniffing at."

"You don't bother to listen good, old man. I already said it once, a few days ago. I know how to make Las Vegas go dark."

"Ha! How would you do that?" Chief asked.

Ernesto's lip curled. "Think! Where does the electrical power come from to light this unworthy town? It comes from Hoover Dam," he answered. "Destroy the dam and you destroy the power."

Tonia might have hooted in ridicule at the crazy thing Ernesto just said, but she was still a little afraid of him. "That's impossible," she told him. "Every school kid in Nevada knows it would take a nuclear blast to even put a crack in the dam. Do you know how much concrete is in Hoover Dam? Enough to build a two-lane highway from New York to San Francisco."

Ernesto growled at her, "It isn't necessary to blow up the whole dam. Just one of the intake towers. That will make it no longer able to generate electrical power. Then all the lights—like the ones those men are fooling with right now—would be gone. Pffffft!" Ernesto made a chopping motion with his hand.

The corner occupied by the four of them—Ernesto,

105

Chief, Tonia and Tiger—seemed even dimmer than usual because of the light concentrated on the stage. It was a week of tech rehearsals, when the lighting director and his crew programmed their new quarter-of-a-million-dollar computer console. Dazzling effects had to be created for each individual number. Just then they were working on the flamenco number, and all the flamenco performers were onstage.

The lighting rehearsal was the one the dancers hated most. They had to stand without moving, wearing full costume and full makeup, while the light technicians tried various combinations of color. That took time, and the lights were hot. They'd already been standing there for twenty minutes—Mona and Casey, the other dancers, and Principe. The only person not standing was Don Filipe, who sat astride his horse. Still the lighting director wasn't satisfied. He tried more yellows, then more blues, then went back to the yellows, while the dancers perspired. Principe grew restless and began to lift one foot after another, which made Stan the carpenter nervous—he hadn't bothered to put down the movable floor protector. Stan winced at each clatter of hoof on hardwood.

"But if you blew up the dam, it isn't just the shows that would go dark," Tonia said. "Everything in Las Vegas would turn off—air conditioning, elevators, streetlights, everything."

"What good is a political statement unless everyone notices it?" Ernesto asked.

"Yeah," Tiger agreed. "It wouldn't be much good if people didn't notice." Tonia gave him a suspicious look.

106

Her brother was either playing a strange game, or else he was beginning to believe that bogus Ernesto.

"Always you talk, talk, talk," Chief told Ernesto. "But you never say how you would do these big things you talk about."

"Don't worry about that, old man. I know how to do it. I study it. First, we get a boat. Then we go out on Lake Mead to the dam, but we can't get all the way up to the dam because it's roped off. No boats can run past the buoys. That's where Tiger comes in."

Tiger turned a little pale. "What would I have to do?"

"When we have reach the buoys, you would jump off the boat and go underwater in the lake wearing your scuba gear. You told me you are a very good scuba diver, no?"

Tiger nodded. "Sort of."

"You would then swim to one of the intake towers, and drop explosives into it," Ernesto said. "That's all."

"Oh, great!" Tonia said. "And Tiger would get blown into little bitty flakes of fish food."

Ernesto's venomous look told Tonia what he thought of her. "The device would work on a timer," he growled. "It would not go off for an hour after Tiger placed it. We would be far away by that time."

Chief pulled thoughtfully at the wrinkled skin around his jaws. "All this talk—boats, explosives, swimming things for Tiger. That sounds like much money. You don't look like a rich man to me."

"Ah, but I have certain . . . associates. Political associates. They provide whatever money is needed, no matter how much."

This guy's been watching too many spy movies on TV, Tonia thought. The way he slinks in and out of shadows—that's straight from old Hitchcock films. "Where did you find these associates?" she asked him. "I didn't think you knew many people around here."

"*They* found *me!*" he answered. "One of these men knew me when I was in pris— I mean, when I was living in the city where I grew up. He search for me, because of my reputation—I have no fear, and I know how to do certain jobs. And you!" He pointed at Chief. "You will help me do this important thing."

Chief stopped plucking his jaw. "What good am I to you? I know nothing about bombs. I don't know how to make a boat go, except a rowboat, and the strength of my body is mostly gone."

Intense, Ernesto answered, "We need you. This political action group is made up of men from all over Latin America. But we must have someone from U. S. of A., someone to represent the poor and oppressed of this place. You would come along as one of the people who have been trampled underfoot by the oppressors."

Chief's frown deepened as he thought about what Ernesto said. After a moment he answered, "That I can understand. I don't say I agree, but I can understand it. But what about the boy? Why should Tiger get mixed up in this thing that could hurt him?"

And what about me, Tonia thought. Why does Chief always worry about Tiger and never about me?

Ernesto moved from beside Chief's chair to where

Tiger sat on a short stairway leading to the upper tier of tables. He knelt before Tiger and put his arm around the boy's shoulder.

"Tiger's understanding is much beyond his years," Ernesto said softly, smiling at him. "He have more social conscience than most grown men. Tiger can be trusted—I need him because of that, and because he is smart and brave."

Tiger's chest visibly swelled. Tonia saw it and was disgusted.

"But the girl . . ." Ernesto whirled to stare at her. "She should be kept out of it. Her we do not need."

"Oh, yes you do," Tonia argued, jumping up to be more emphatic. She was needed most of all—that is, if anything ever came of all this bizarre talk—to go along and look out for that silly Tiger and poor old Chief. She said, "Tiger can't get in and out of his scuba gear by himself. It's too heavy for him. I'm the only person who knows how to help him with it. So if you need Tiger, you need me too."

"Hang in there for just a few more minutes, boys and girls," the lighting director shouted. "I think I've almost got it."

Ernesto spoke softly. "They will leave the stage soon. I must be there when the horse come off, or Don Filipe will hit me again with his horsewhip. Tiger, here is what you do: make a list of all the scuba gear you need. Money is not to be a concern; my group will provide all that is necessary. Write it down on the list, and give it to me tomorrow."

109

"I'll write it," Tonia said. "You'd never be able to read Tiger's handwriting."

"All right, kids," Jocko called over the mike, "thank you for your patience. Looks like we've got the lights worked out for the flamenco number. Take a half-hour break. When you come back, everyone in the barndance number will go on stage for a tech rehearsal. Full costume."

"I must leave," Ernesto said, disappearing into shadow. "Remember the list, Tiger. Bring it tomorrow."

"We have to go, too," Tonia said. She pulled Tiger's arm. "We have to get into our costumes and makeup."

"Wait a minute. Wait a minute," Tiger said, holding back. "I . . . I don't know what . . . Shouldn't we talk about . . . ?"

"The man who calls himself Ernesto," Chief finished. "That man speaks like a devil. A dust devil. Out in the desert are things called dust devils—whirlwinds that blow hot air around and around in circles, until at last they disappear into nothing. I think Ernesto is only a dust devil. And yet—what if he means his big words about the dam?"

Anxious to go downstairs to the dressing room, afraid to be late for the tech rehearsal, Tonia hesitated only because Chief seemed really concerned. "If you think he means it, then we ought to go to the police," she said. "But I think he's lying. He's just dreaming up things to make himself look big, because he's such a low, slimy fungus. Ernesto's so low, he could jump off a piece of paper and die of old age on the way down."

"Don't talk that way!" Tiger yelled, punching her shoulder. "We're not going to the police, you hear? Forget that! I'm going to do what Ernesto says, and make that list of scuba gear. I'll ask Heather to help me with it after we get home tonight."

"Oh, spaz down," Tonia snapped. "And quit hitting me or I'll tell Dad."

For once Chief didn't stop their quarrel. He was thinking too hard to pay attention to them. "Go to the police," he muttered. "Is that a wise thing? A man shouldn't be arrested just for talking. And the police might deport Ernesto—Don Filipe always threatens to have him deported. Does Ernesto speak true, or does he only make up big talk out of hate? We must wait and see."

"Come on," Tonia said, yanking Tiger's arm. "It takes me a long time to put on my makeup."

"That's because there's so much of you," Tiger answered.

Tonia tripped him, and felt great satisfaction to hear Tiger's yelp of pain when he landed on his knees.

She stuck out her tongue and pretended to gag. "This sign means," she told Chief, "that Tiger makes me puke."

Nine

Heather's body made Tonia's want to shrivel up and hide.

Heather was a serious swimmer, spending two-thirds of her waking hours in water. Mornings she instructed scuba at the University of Nevada at Las Vegas; afternoons she lifeguarded and taught little kids to swim in the condo pool. Whenever she could work it in, Heather swam laps—three miles' worth each day in the university pool. It was the laps that made Heather's body look better than Wonder Woman's.

"You're nice and trim these days, Tonia," Heather said.

"What!" Tonia couldn't believe that, coming from Heather, the bikini bod-goddess. "I'm not trim. I'm fat."

"Yeah, you're still plenty overweight," Heather agreed. "But you've firmed up considerably. You're in a lot better physical shape than you used to be. I bet your stamina's increased, hasn't it? I bet you can run upstairs twice as fast as you used to."

Tonia nodded. It was true that physical exertion seemed easier for her than it ever had. But as for looks, she still considered herself Tonia the Tub.

"What we're here for," Tiger said, wanting to divert Heather's attention to himself, "is a list of scuba equipment. If I wanted to go diving in Lake Mead, what would I need?"

"Hey, wait a minute, guy." Heather's hand flew up in a forbidding gesture. "What's this about diving at Lake Mead?"

"Well, someday I plan to," Tiger declared. "With all the money I'm going to earn being in this show at the WestAmerica, I could buy myself the best scuba gear made. So I'd like you to help me make up a list, Heather."

"Sit down," Heather commanded Tiger. "You too, Tonia—I want you to listen hard so you can repeat to your father everything I'm going to say, in case Tiger doesn't take me seriously."

Heather had been born a redhead. Her short, curly hair was naturally auburn, but sun and chlorine had bleached the different strands to every imaginable hue of red. Tonia had heard that redheads had tempers, and Heather seemed about to get really angry. Tonia and Tiger lowered themselves onto webbed lounge chairs designed so people could lean back and relax, but since Heather looked so threatening, they didn't relax. They sat gingerly on the edges of the chairs.

"Now pay attention, and listen good," Heather said. "Tiger, you are not to attempt to dive in Lake Mead. It's dangerous. It's illegal. And it can be fatal."

113

"What do you mean, illegal?" Tiger challenged her. "Lots of people scuba in Lake Mead."

"Only after they've been certified. Do you know what that means?"

Tiger started to nod, then shook his head. "Not altogether, I guess."

"It means you have to get tons more hours of scuba instruction than you've had. The drills have to be taught to you by a certified instructor, which I'm not—I'm only a teaching assistant. Then you have to go out into open water—not in a swimming pool—and demonstrate all your skills to the instructor. That's how you get certified as a diver. And unless you can prove you're certified, it's illegal for any dive shop to fill your air tanks."

Tiger slumped on the edge of the patio chair. "They sure make it tough," he muttered.

"You bet they do," Heather said. "They make it tough because diving is dangerous. All kinds of things can go wrong—for one, your equipment can fail. That's why you never go diving alone. You always go with a buddy."

"What else can go wrong?" Tonia asked. She wanted to remember everything Heather was saying so she could report it to her father if Tiger ever got any wild ideas.

Heather answered, "Another danger is vertigo. That's the effect of water pressure on the body. Different people get it at different depths, some at maybe sixty feet, and others maybe not till they've gone down a hundred and fifty feet. It depends on the person's physiology."

"What's vertigo?" Tiger asked.

"It means you don't know which direction is up. You get confused, like you're drunk. That's an extra reason why you always dive with a buddy, because if your buddy notices you acting weird, he can take you up to the surface. But vertigo's not the worst thing that can happen."

Impressed by Heather's intensity, Tiger wanted to know the worst. "What is?"

"An air embolism," Heather told them. "If you panic and hold your breath, you can burst the alveoli in your lungs, and you'll drown in your own blood." She let that sink in before she added, "The way to avoid an air embolism is to breathe constantly through your regulator, and never hold your breath while you're diving. If you hold your breath, you can get into fatal trouble."

Stricken, Tiger looked at Tonia, who stared back, horrified. Both of them remembered the day in May when Tiger tricked Tonia by holding his breath to play dead.

"Have I scared you?" Heather asked.

"Yes!" they both shouted.

"Good! I'm glad, because if you ever did anything dumb, Tiger, like trying to dive in Lake Mead, I'd feel responsible. After all, I'm the one who let you borrow my gear to fool around in the bottom of the pool," Heather said. "I taught you a few rudimentary basics about diving because I thought you were responsible

115

enough to handle it. But if you ever tried to dive in open water . . . God, I'd . . . ! You hear me? Don't you dare! Not till you've learned enough to become certified."

"I couldn't anyway, could I?" Tiger asked. "You said no place will fill a diver's air tanks unless the diver proves he's certified."

"Oh, people find ways to get around that, I'm afraid," Heather said. "Which is unfortunate, because those are the people who end up drowned."

Tiger shivered, although the temperature at poolside was a hundred and twelve, according to the big circular thermometer that hung on the wire fence. He asked quietly, "Tonia, did you bring the pencil and paper?"

"Yeah, why? Don't tell me you still want that list!"

Tiger turned to Heather. "Don't worry, I won't try to dive in any open water. I'm not totally stupid. But this will just be like a . . . like a wish list. You know, a game. If you had all the money in the world, what would be the best scuba equipment you could buy?"

"Oh, a game." Heather relaxed, and her eyes became lively. "Let's see," she said. "With all the money in the world, what would I buy? There are fancy Lycra wet suits, and great new buoyancy systems, and the usual fins and all that necessary stuff. But you know what I'd really love to have if I were unbearably rich? A DPV."

"A DPV?" Tiger asked. "What's that?"

"It stands for diver propulsion vehicle. It's like a little torpedo, with handles." Heather grinned, enjoying her fantasy. "They're really, really neat—you hang onto one end and it pulls you through the water a lot faster

116

and a lot farther than you can swim by yourself. You see them on *Jacques Cousteau* sometimes. Only, the cheapest one costs about eighteen hundred dollars. Still, if I were incredibly rich . . ." Heather leaned back, smiled, and stretched her arms above her head so that her bikini-clad body showed every muscle separation, yet still looked awesomely feminine. "Do I have to spend all my money on scuba stuff?" she asked.

"Write that down—a DPV," Tiger told Tonia. "Now, what kind of wet suit would I need?"

Heather paused. "You seem awful serious, Tiger. This is only pretend, isn't it?"

"Sure," he agreed. "Only pretend."

.   .   .

"Did you bring the list?" Ernesto hissed from the shadows.

"Yeah. Here it is. I got it." Tiger moved toward the wall drapery that half concealed Ernesto. Tonia followed, not wanting to miss anything.

"Boy, the stuff on this list would cost a fortune if you really bought it," Tiger told Ernesto, "but . . ."

"I told you! Cost is of no matter! My associates have a big supply of money that come from a secret place even I don't know where is at." Ernesto grabbed the paper from Tiger's hand and pushed it into the pocket of his tight blue jeans. "I can stay only for one minute. Don Filipe watches me like the evil eye to see that I am always with the horse. Since the day Principe broke away from us, Don Filipe no longer trust me. So call the old man over here. Quickly!"

"I'll get him!" Tonia ran to Chief's chair, whispered

in his ear, and helped him to his feet. He came as quickly as he could, but Chief could never move with much speed.

"This is what we plan to do," Ernesto announced as soon as Chief reached him. "The four of us will meet, then go backstage through the door that go outside. One of my associates . . . a very important man . . . will wait there with a van. The scuba gear will be inside it. Behind the van, a boat will be . . . what is the word? Hitch! Are you listening, old man?" Ernesto asked sharply.

Startled, Chief nodded.

"Pay attention, all of you," Ernesto snapped. "We will drive to Boulder Beach, and launch the boat there. We will steer the boat out to the buoys. It is there that Tiger goes into the water. Any questions?"

He'd bombarded them with such rapid-fire instructions that Tonia and Chief couldn't think of any questions, but Tiger asked, "When is all this going to happen?"

"Monday morning," Ernesto replied.

"Monday morning!" Tonia cried. "We can't do it then. Dress rehearsals begin Monday."

"Do you still not understand?" Ernesto asked her. "There will be no electrical power, so there will be no show. So the rehearsal of dresses matters nothing!"

Tonia had no answer to that. It wasn't until Ernesto had gone that she allowed herself a tiny, scared giggle about "rehearsal of dresses."

.   .   .

"What'll we do?" Tonia asked Chief.

"If only I had the wisdom of Father Owl, to tell

whether Ernesto speaks the truth or has a head full of imaginings. What good is it to be so old if a man has no wisdom?" Chief regretted. "Even when I was young, I found it hard to judge a man's truthfulness, because I believed that everyone was good in his heart. I thought that insight would come to me when I grew old. But here I am, weak in body, weak in mind. . . ."

Tonia looked at Tiger. Sometimes, without any words, each knew what the other was thinking. Tonia went to one side of Chief, Tiger to the other, and they both hugged him. "We think you're really smart," Tiger told him.

"We know you'll decide what we should do," Tonia said. "After all, we're only kids—we don't know anything. You've lived so long that you know a whole lot more than we do. So you tell us—should we go to the police?"

"No! No police!" Tiger shouted.

"Hmmph!" Chief snorted, and sat up straighter. "One thing I know for certain. Most police don't believe much of what an Indian tells them. And I think the police don't believe many words of children, either. The kind of work that policemen do turns them into doubters of human beings."

"I bet you're right," Tiger said.

"I wouldn't blame the police for not believing us," Tonia said. "I don't believe what Ernesto says myself. I think he's a complete whack. Totally crazy."

"He's not!" Tiger cried.

"Sure he's crazy. All that talk about blowing up Hoover Dam, and some big organization . . . that has

119

to come from a sick mind. Ernesto probably sees little green men following him, too."

"Hush. Hush, children. Tonia, you should think about this: a man who is really crazy can cause much more damage than a man who is not crazy at all."

Tonia mulled that over, and had to agree. "Chief, you really are wise."

"So!" Chief sat up even straighter. "A plan is coming into my head," he said slowly. "It's a picture, like a dream. This is what it looks like—Monday morning, I will not be here, yet I will be here."

"Huh?"

"He means he'll be hiding where Ernesto can't see him," Tonia told Tiger. "Right, Chief?"

"Right. You can tell Ernesto this—that is, if Ernesto is really going to act out his dust-devil plan. Tell him I telephoned you to say my truck had a flat tire while I was driving in from the reservation. Tell him the garage man says he doesn't know how long it will take to fix the tire. Tell him I will drive straight to Boulder Beach and meet you there."

Tiger looked puzzled. "We're supposed to tell Ernesto all this, and all the time you'll be right here, Chief?"

"Watching you." Light came into Chief's eyes. "And stalking Ernesto. He won't see me, and you won't see me. Who is better at stalking his prey than an Indian? If this plan Ernesto talks about turns out to be true, and not just a wild imagining, I'll stalk him like the warrior I once was. I'll stalk his van with my truck, but he won't know I'm behind him. When the van, with you in it, reaches Boulder City, I'll drive straight to the police. Then I'll bring the police to the dock at Boulder Beach, before Ernesto and the very important man can get the boat into the water."

"And then . . ." Tonia began, excited, "the police will catch them with all the evidence. The boat, the scuba gear, and the bomb."

Tiger looked worried.

"Unless the whole thing is only a loco dream from Ernesto's head," Chief said. "In that case, on Monday we just rehearse the dresses, like we're supposed to."

Ten

"Do you see Chief anywhere?" Tiger asked on Monday morning. He spoke quietly, even though no one could hear him over the sound of the stage sets being rolled into place.

Tonia answered, "No, but I didn't expect to. He said we wouldn't be able to see him. I wonder how long he's going to keep hiding before he decides this whole thing is a big fake."

"You won't think it's a fake much longer," Tiger muttered. "There's Ernesto."

Crouching behind a railing, Ernesto motioned for Tiger and Tonia to come to him. The dark clothing he wore made him hard to notice. When they reached him, he asked, "Where's the old man?"

"Uh . . . uh . . ."

Tiger was the world's worst actor, so Tonia had to take over. "Chief called just a little while ago," she answered. "His truck had a flat tire. He said for us to go without him, and he'll meet us at Boulder Beach."

Ernesto let out a stream of words that sounded as if

they might be Spanish swear words, but Tonia couldn't tell for sure.

"Come then," Ernesto said angrily. "Follow me."

It was beginning to seem that Ernesto's plan might be more than wild talk. Still, he could just be a crazy person, Tonia thought, but if that were true, who wanted to follow a maniac out of a nice, secure building to heaven-knew-where? That was the moment to yell for help—to Mona, to Casey, to anyone. One loud shriek, and the whole cast would stop talking, would turn around to see what was the matter. But Tonia couldn't bring herself to let out that shriek. Everything in the showroom looked so normal, so ordinary for a Monday morning. No one had laid a hand on Tonia; no one held a gun on her. If she screamed, everyone would think *she* was the crazy person.

Then Tiger moved to follow Ernesto, so Tonia had no choice except to follow her brother, to protect him. And Chief could be counted on to protect them both, by bringing the police if this thing really happened. She looked behind to see if Chief was visible, but couldn't find him. "Dummy," she told herself, "you're not supposed to see him."

Ernesto didn't lead them backstage, as he'd said he would, but through a hotel corridor that emerged onto a different part of the parking lot. Beyond the door, the bright August sunlight dazzled Tonia for a moment, so that she had to shade her eyes to see. What she saw blasted away her last doubts.

A chocolate-colored van waited with its motor running. Behind the van, on a trailer, sat a large boat, its

123

white sides and chrome rails gleaming in the sun, its propeller blades idle but powerful-looking.

"In," Ernesto told them, jerking his thumb toward the open side door of the van. When Tiger hesitated, Ernesto grabbed him by the arm and half lifted him into the van. Tonia followed quickly, without protest, because her skin crawled at the thought of Ernesto touching her. This was real, all right; this whole big scary monster deal that she hadn't believed in was turning out to be real. As the van door slid shut behind her, she had to remind herself that Chief was watching everything that happened.

Ernesto entered through the front door and sat next to the driver. Immediately the van jerked forward, knocking Tonia and Tiger off balance. Since the middle row of seats had been removed, they stumbled to the very back of the van to sit down.

From there, Tonia peered forward to try to get a look at the driver, who must be the important person Ernesto had talked about. The man wasn't tall, and the bucket seat on the driver's side came up high enough that she could see only little bits of him, like pieces of a kaleidoscope image that didn't fit together in a clear whole.

He wore a Greek fisherman's cap, and wraparound, mirror-lensed sunglasses. When he turned to say something to Ernesto, Tonia glimpsed his cheek—the palest, pinkest skin she'd ever seen on a grown man. A neat gray beard hugged the bottom of his pink chin. From the little she could see, he looked like someone's kindly grandfather.

Tiger pointed to the length of floor between the front

124

and back seats. It was filled with boxes marked *Neptune Diving Supplies.* "I think I'm getting sick," he whispered. "What if I really have to dive in Lake Mead?"

"Don't worry. Remember Chief." Tonia twisted to look out the back window, craning her neck to see over the high bulk of the boat, trying to spot an orange and white, beat-up Chevrolet pickup truck, the kind Chief told her he drove. She couldn't see much of anything.

As they turned the corner from Tropicana Avenue onto Boulder Highway, Tiger began to examine each box on the floor. "That one could hold a wet suit," he murmured so that only Tonia heard him. "That other one's probably a compressed air tank, because it looks like it's been packed real carefully. That wooden box I can't figure out, but the big box . . ." He pointed. "I don't have to guess about that, because it says it right on the side. *Diver Propulsion Vehicle.* He really did it. He really got it!"

Tonia's heart pounded so hard it felt as though her breastbone would be bruised from the inside. "I can't believe this is really happening," she said. "How did things go this far?"

"I wonder if Chief's behind us," Tiger said, straining to see out the back window.

Suddenly Ernesto's seat swiveled all the way around to face them. "Why do you keep looking out the back like that?" he asked.

"Uh . . . uh . . ."

"We're admiring the boat," Tonia said, coming to Tiger's rescue again. She was trying to sound normal, but her voice shook. "It's really a beauty, that boat.

125

Does it have a name? You know, people usually name their boats, like they name their kids and dogs and cats."

"I think it's called the *Hot Fudge*," Ernesto replied. "What difference does it make?"

"The *Hot Fudge*—that's cute. Does that mean they only use it on Sundays?"

Her giggle dwindled to a faint whimper. What was the matter with her, making terrible jokes at a time like this?

The van made a sudden left turn that caused Ernesto's seat to swivel toward the passenger door. As it did, the wooden box that had been wedged beneath the seat slid sideways, and came to rest against the doorpost only a few feet from Tonia and Tiger. At the same instant, both of them noticed the words imprinted on the side of the box. *Water Gel Dynamite. Handle With Care.* The van straightened, and the box slid toward them.

"Ernesto!" Tonia screamed. "Is that really dynamite?"

He turned around and laughed at her. "What do you think?" Then he grew serious. "Why do you act surprised? Did you think we were just going to Lake Mead for a little picnic? I don't fool around, *muchacha*. What I say, I mean."

"But . . . but . . . shouldn't you tie it down or something? The box is sliding all over the floor. It might explode!"

"Dynamite don't explode all that easy." Ernesto's lips curled a bit because Tonia was so obviously afraid.

He slid down in his seat, pulled the box toward him with his foot, and began to kick the wooden sides. Slowly, with the heavy heel of his boot, he kicked the box again and again. Thud. Thud. Thud. All the while he stared into Tonia's eyes.

"No!" she moaned. "Don't do that!"

The driver spoke to Ernesto sharply, in Spanish. He stopped kicking the box and looked sullen.

"What's . . . his name?" Tiger stuttered, gesturing toward the driver, trying to get everyone's mind away from the dynamite box that moved toward them, then away.

"El Gavilán," Ernesto answered. His mood changed again; he was always friendly with Tiger. "It means 'The Hawk.' In the political action group, we don't use our real names."

"Uh . . . does The Hawk know we're not on Boulder Highway anymore?" Tiger asked.

"He knows," Ernesto said. "We are on Lakeshore Road."

"We could get to Boulder Beach quicker if we stayed on Boulder Highway," Tiger told him.

"We're not going to Boulder Beach. We're going to Callville Bay."

"What!" Tiger nearly yelled. "You don't want to go to Callville. I heard that Callville Bay was hit really hard by that big storm we had. It's a real mess. All the ramps were wiped out. You'd have to launch the boat off the shore."

"Exactly," Ernesto said. "So hardly anyone will be there. That means hardly anyone will notice us."

127

"What about Chief?" Tonia wailed. "Chief is supposed to meet us at Boulder—"

Tiger grabbed her arm and dug his nails into her flesh. "Shut up and hype down," he growled at her.

Ernesto shrugged. "The old man will just have to miss his big chance to get his name in the papers." Turning his seat, he faced forward again.

"You nearly blew it," Tiger whispered, poking Tonia with his elbow after Ernesto no longer watched them.

"Don't say 'blew it'! Don't *say* that!" she sniffled, as the dynamite box moved toward them a few more inches.

"You know what I mean. You're so wired you're saying stupid things. Just take it easy. Chief will follow us no matter where we go, so it doesn't matter that the plans got changed to Callville."

Tonia closed her eyes and clenched her whole body to get herself under control. After a moment she whispered back, "Even if he finds us, there are no police at Callville."

"Callville has park rangers. They're as good as police. Chief will bring the rangers right after we get there," Tiger told her, as though he were sure. But he wasn't sure about anything. In his entire life, he'd never felt so confused.

.   .   .

He was still good at it, as old as he was. Even though the boy and the girl had turned around several times, they hadn't been able to see him. Chief might have enjoyed himself if he hadn't been so concerned for the safety of the boy and the girl.

128

Ernesto's talk had turned out to be true. The old man blamed himself for not sensing the difference between the hot, wild talk of a dreamer and the cold, dangerous talk of a hater. What good was it to be so old if he still couldn't read men's hearts? He shook his head inside the orange and white 1971 Chevrolet pickup as it shimmied down Boulder Highway. A large diesel rig in front of his truck hid it from the occupants of the boat-pulling van in front of the diesel.

At Russell Road the van and boat pulled through the intersection, beating the red traffic light. But the diesel stopped, so Chief had to stop, too. It didn't matter; he'd catch up to the van at the next traffic light. The light turned green, the diesel rumbled forward, and Chief's foot pressed down on the gas pedal.

The engine chugged, chugged again, and died. Chief turned the key, but although the starter whined, the motor would not start. Horns honked behind him. Chief's hands began to shake. Again and again he turned the ignition key. The engine refused to turn over.

Chief got out of the truck. Cars swerved around him. Some drivers blasted their horns, some shook their fists. Chief didn't know what to do; he'd grown up on horseback, and understood very little about engines. Uncertain, he stood on Boulder Highway as the passing motorists yelled at him.

Across the highway, another pickup stopped along the edge of the road. A young Indian got out and raced across the highway, dodging traffic as gracefully as an antelope outrunning dogs. His black hair was long; it rose and fell in layers as he ran, but when he reached

Chief, each hair had gone back neatly into place. The young man was not even out of breath.

"You got trouble with your truck, Grandfather?" he asked. The name "Grandfather" was used in respect; Chief had never before seen the young Indian, who was from a different tribe.

"Do you know how to open the hood?" the young man asked Chief.

"That much I know." Chief climbed inside and released the hood latch.

The young man jumped onto the front bumper to peer at the Chevrolet's insides. "I see what's wrong," he said, fooling with something out of Chief's line of vision. "Try her again, Grandfather."

Chief turned the ignition key, and the motor jumped to life. He smiled widely in thanks, ready to go on, but the young man stood with his hand on the open window ledge.

"Better pull over to the curb for a minute, Grandfather," he said.

"I can't! I have to hurry fast."

"Your truck might stall again at the next light," the youth said. "I got to show you how to fix her when she stalls, or you ain't going nowhere."

Chief studied the face. He could not be mistaken this time—it was an honest, friendly face he saw, a face that would not lie. Chief pulled over into a nearby parking lot. Before the young man even reached him, the engine chugged and once again died.

"See," the young man said, "if you try to start her again, she won't start. Come out, and I'll show you

130

what you must do. Only, Grandfather, this time when I start her, I think you should take her straight to a garage. You want me to go with you?"

"What is the matter with her?" Chief asked.

"Carburetor trouble." He opened the hood and showed Chief how to take off the air cleaner cover and insert a pencil to hold open the butterfly valve. "It'll start now," he said. "After it starts, you have to take out the pencil and put back the cover of the air cleaner, then close the hood, and you're on your way. If you can keep from stopping, she'll probably run, but if you stop, she'll stall, and you'll have to open the valve each time to start her."

Chief knew he could no longer find the brown van that pulled the boat. He would have to go straight to the Boulder City police. "I thank you with my heart," he told the young Indian. "What is it people call you?"

"Bobby." The young man grinned. "I'm from the reservation at Yuma. I started out at four this morning so I could get to Vegas before it gets too hot, because my truck don't have air condition. So here I am. Ain't I, Grandfather? Ain't this Las Vegas?"

"It is."

"I come here to be a musician. I play guitar and I sing real good. Someday I'll be famous. Then you can say Bobby Calamity helped you with your truck, once."

Chief looked at the handsome young man, so confident. He told him, "I cannot offer you a worthy return for your kindness to me. Except for this advice: Forget the singing in Las Vegas. Go to a gas station and get yourself a job as a mechanic. Las Vegas has too many singers and not enough good mechanics. But you are young, and you will not heed my good advice, so tomorrow, come to the WestAmerica showroom. You will find me there, and I'll try to help you."

The young Indian didn't believe the old one, but he smiled and said, "If I ain't already a big star by then, Grandfather, I'll come."

.   .   .

Chief was right; he couldn't find the brown van. All along the road to Boulder City he looked for it, but he'd lost too much time over the carburetor trouble. When he got to Boulder City, the town built to house the people who'd made Hoover Dam, he asked directions to the police station.

"What can I do for you, sir?" the officer at the desk asked. He looked the way all policemen look: large, ruddy, handsome, well-groomed, and expressionless. His face stayed expressionless while Chief told him about the terrorists, the bomb, and the children.

"Sir, would you repeat your story to these other officers?" the desk officer requested politely, so Chief had to go through the whole thing again.

"We'll take a run down to the harbor and check it out," the patrolmen said. "Why don't you drive down with us, sir?"

From the back seat of the police car, Chief looked out at the brown, withered hills that had once been home to his people. Then he saw blue water. They were nearing Lake Mead.

"You say they were going to launch the boat out of Boulder Beach?" one of the patrolmen asked.

"Yes. Where is that harbor?"

"Over there."

Chief's heart sank. He saw twelve docks in the harbor, each with dozens of boats attached like baby pups suckling a mother dog.

"Lots of boats around here," the patrolmen said. "Can you describe the one we're looking for?"

"It's white," Chief told them.

"They're all white, sir."

The men were kind; they even let Chief use their binoculars to look for the van, the boat, the children, and Ernesto. He couldn't find them. The policemen didn't say an unkind word, but Chief imagined that they were thinking: "Another old, useless, drunken Indian." They were not right about the drunken part, but about old and useless, they were altogether right, Chief believed.

"Don't you want us to drive you back to your truck?" they asked him, but Chief said no, he'd wait at the docks for a while.

They left him standing there, staring at the deep blue waters of Lake Mead.

Eleven

Ernesto slid open the side door. "Get into the boat," he told Tiger and Tonia.

"It isn't even in the water yet," Tonia protested. "It's still hitched to the back of the van."

"Do what I tell you!" Ernesto didn't shout, but he sounded so menacing that Tonia and Tiger almost tumbled out of the van in their hurry to obey. Beyond Ernesto's shoulder, Tonia could see the aluminum-sided Callville Ranger Station. Now would be the time to make a run for it—the park rangers would find all the evidence they needed in the van.

But Ernesto stood right next to them as he shepherded Tiger and Tonia around the back of the trailer. And The Hawk was right behind them as they climbed the short ladder into the boat.

In the stern, The Hawk stopped to remove his Greek fisherman's cap and wipe his head. Except for the little tuft of beard on his chin, he had no hair at all. The top of his head was as smooth and pink as an Easter egg.

After he put the cap back on, he stood for a moment and stared at Tonia. At least she thought he was staring, but she couldn't be sure—his eyes were invisible behind the sunglasses. She could only see herself, reflected in the mirror lenses: a chubby, terrified girl dressed ridiculously in a lavender leotard and purple dance tights, probably the most bizarre boating outfit in the history of Lake Mead. Would anyone wonder why she was dressed that way? Notice me, someone, she prayed. Girls don't wear dance suits to go boating on a hot day. Notice that something's wrong with this scene!

The few other people along the shoreline of Callville Bay were intent upon getting their own boats into the water, and paid no attention to the *Hot Fudge* or its crew. After all the diving equipment had been transferred to the boat, Ernesto backed the van and trailer downhill into the bay. The Hawk started the engine then; the propellers churned water with a slurping sound. Tonia didn't realize the boat was off the trailer until she saw Ernesto drive the van uphill to park it.

As soon as Ernesto jumped aboard, the *Hot Fudge* headed for open water, speeding up until a V-shaped wake cut the surface of Lake Mead behind them. Rainbows danced in the spray from the wake; the drops of water reflected sunlight the way sequins on showgirls' costumes reflect theatrical lights—in brilliant primal colors.

Tonia and Tiger sat in the stern, where hot wind whipped their faces in continuous puffs. Since The Hawk didn't need help to operate the boat, Ernesto came into the stern and sat next to Tiger, crowding

Tonia so much she got up and moved to a bench along the side.

"Here, put these on while we ride," Ernesto told Tiger. He handed him a pair of sunglasses. "Glare from water will make your eyes hurt, so I bought these for you."

"What about me?" Tonia asked.

Ernesto didn't answer. His look told her that to him, she was as worthless as spit.

They left behind Callville, with its white Ranger Station and its fringe of green trees. On either side of the lake, jagged, rough-edged peaks rose brown out of the blue waters. The peaks were the tops of whole mountains, the only parts that remained visible after Lake Mead had filled the canyons to make the enormous reservoir.

"How long will it take to get to the dam?" Tiger asked, talking loud because of the motor noise.

"About half an hour." Ernesto spoke loudly, too. "That gives me time to explain to you what you have to do. But first, I want to tell you that it's important what you do—to make people aware of injustice. That a boy your age cares so much will make a big impression on people. And the best part is, no one will get hurt by what we are doing."

"Are you sure about that?" Tiger asked.

"Absolute sure. After the bomb goes off inside the intake tower, it will wreck the hoist mechanism. Then the big intake gate will seal shut. No water can get in to power the turbines, so Las Vegas will receive no

136

electricity. Very simple. Very effective. And no one gets hurt."

"I thought there were four intake towers," Tiger said.

"Right. But we are interested only in the tower that supplies water to the generators for Las Vegas. I show you which one that is."

Tiger looked at the lake, which was only a little choppy. Not enough to trouble a diver, but Tiger was plenty concerned. "How will I put the explosive into the tower?" he asked.

"Not hard. Not hard at all." Ernesto knelt on the bottom of the boat and untied the cord from around the box marked *Diver Propulsion Vehicle*. He removed the top to reveal an orange, torpedolike device with two handles, one on either side at the back.

"I can't work that thing!" Tiger said, his voice going higher. "I never even saw one before now."

Ernesto's voice lowered as Tiger's rose. Soothingly, he said, "It's so easy. See, in front of the left handle is this little switch that make it go." He pulled back the switch for a second, and a propeller at the back of the vehicle did a few slow turns. "In front of the right handle is the light switch, so you can see under water." When Ernesto turned it on, a beam of light illuminated the inside front of the packing box. "The light switch will stay on by itself. The power switch you have to hold all the time, or the vehicle will stop." Ernesto demonstrated. "See? Hold the power switch with the forefinger while the left hand grips the handle."

Tiger got down beside Ernesto. "That's neat," he

137

said, experimenting with the power switch. "How do you steer it?"

"Point it whatever way you wish to go. It can go three miles an hour underwater. Just hang on, and it will take you forward, much faster than you could swim. And you don't get tired."

Tiger stroked the bright orange side of the diver propulsion vehicle. "So okay. Say I'm in the water with this thing. What do I do?"

Tiger had begun to seem so interested that Tonia grew alarmed. He couldn't just be pretending—Tiger wasn't that good an actor.

"You dive down a few feet. Not so many—maybe twenty. Enough that no one can see you from above. Follow your compass directly southwest till you reach the first intake tower on the Nevada side," Ernesto told him. "That's four hundred fifty feet from the buoy where you enter the lake. Not such a long swim."

"If this thing goes three miles an hour, to get there it will take me . . ."

"Only a couple minutes to reach the tower. It will be fun, and you get to keep the vehicle afterwards. When you reach the tower, you dive a hundred feet down, to where the gate is."

"A hundred feet! I've never been deeper than ten."

Ernesto's hand lightly pressed Tiger's shoulder. "Nothing to worry. Ten feet, a hundred feet—once you're underwater, there is not much difference. When the intake gate opens, you throw the dynamite inside and swim away. . . ."

"Wait a minute!" Tonia yelled. "When that huge gate

opens and all the water rushes inside, it'll suck Tiger right into the tower. Tiger along with the dynamite."

Ernesto snarled at her, "Not true! A steel rack keeps the debris from going through."

"Oh! So now you're calling my brother debris!"

"Shut up!" Ernesto cried, and Tonia did, because he looked as if he would gladly trash her. He turned to Tiger again and asked pleasantly, "Do you have more questions?"

Tiger asked, "If I'm holding onto the diver vehicle with both hands, how will I hold the dynamite?"

Ernesto's smile flashed. "Smart question! But you worry too much, Tiger. Can't you tell by now that I think of everything?" He raised the seat cushion on the bench opposite Tonia and rummaged in the storage area underneath, until he came up with a crowbar. With the narrow edge, Ernesto pried up the lid of the wooden box.

"This is it." He spoke almost reverently as he pointed to the bomb in the box. It lay in chips of styrofoam: three sticks of water-gel dynamite, each two and a half inches in diameter and a foot long, tied together with plastic bands. At one end, a blasting cap and a small clock had been fastened. "This is set to explode after we return to shore," Ernesto said, "so no one will know who did it. Or why. They'll learn when the letter I mail this morning reach the newspaper."

Tiger leaned away from the box. "You're sure it can't go off before that?"

"No worry. Trust me."

They were passing Boulder Beach, which lay far to

their right. Tonia searched the water for any white with green stripe Park Service launches, but couldn't see even one. The lake was quiet; few sportsmen came out in their boats on Monday mornings.

"You still didn't answer. How am I supposed to manage the dynamite while I'm holding the diver vehicle?" Tiger asked.

"With this." Ernesto held up two pieces of pliable rubber tubing, eighteen inches long. "We will tie the explosives to your leg with this."

"Ernesto, he's only little! He only weighs eighty pounds . . . !" Tonia wailed.

"Eighty-two," Tiger corrected her.

"So how's he supposed to manage an at-pack, an air tank, and that . . . whatever-you-call-it diver vehicle, with a bomb on his leg?"

"Everything weighs less in water," Ernesto answered, speaking to Tiger rather than Tonia. "You will have no trouble. I checked with experts."

They passed through a narrow corridor where the rock walls on either side looked close enough to touch. Suddenly, as the boat emerged from the corridor, the high curve of Hoover Dam shone white ahead of them.

"There it is," Tiger said.

The Hawk steered the boat all the way up to a string of buoys that marked the point past which boats weren't allowed to go, then turned off the engine.

Like four giant white salt and pepper shakers, the intake towers stood in front of the dam, two on the Nevada side of the lake, two on the Arizona side. Each tower rose a hundred feet into the air; the rest of it, the

140

lower three-fourths, was submerged beneath the lake's surface. The nearest tower on the right, on the Nevada side, didn't look at all distant from where the boat bobbed next to the buoys.

"That shouldn't be so hard to reach," Tiger said.

Ernesto slid an arm around Tiger's shoulder. "You know I would never ask you to do a thing that would put you into danger," he said. "Now it is time to get into your gear." He knelt to open the final two boxes.

One held a full wet suit, booties, hood, fins, mask, regulator, console, and air hoses, all carefully packed. The other contained a tank-mounted bouyancy system called an at-pack, to be worn on the diver's back. Each piece of gear was brand-new and top of the line.

"Gol, look at that," Tiger breathed. "They're even the right size."

"Of course. I'm a careful planner. Put them on quick," Ernesto said. "Sister, you help him, like you say you know how to. Hurry!" He checked his watch.

Tonia looked around for a Park Service boat, for any kind of boat, for any kind of human help. No one was around. Not even a fish jumped to ruffle the surface of the lake. Everything seemed unreal, like a play on a stage. Except part of the cast was missing—Chief and the police!

"I said hurry!" Ernesto yelled at her.

"I can't do this stuff!" she yelled back. "I don't know how to attach the air tank to the at-pack. Heather always did that part."

"I can manage it," Tiger told them. He worked slowly and meticulously, checking each valve and connection again and again as he filled the balloon inside the at-pack. It seemed to take forever. Ernesto paced the limited space of the boat, while The Hawk smoked a pipe and studied the dam, looking more than ever like someone's grandpa.

"Now Tonia can help me," Tiger said at last. He held up the dive suit; it was designed like a fancy pair of longjohns, navy blue through the body and legs, bright yellow in the shoulders. "She can help me put this on."

He's really going to go through with it, Tonia thought. Oh Chief, please come. Someone—help us! Don't let this go any farther!

The lake stayed quiet, peaceful. No sound of a motor boat disturbed the stillness. The nearest sign of life was on top of the dam, where cars and trucks, toy-sized in the distance, crossed between Nevada and Arizona.

"I don't see how we can do this without Chief," Tonia said, stalling. "The whole idea was to have Chief represent the poor and oppressed. Tiger and I can't represent the poor and oppressed—we're rich, spoiled kids, sort of. We'd give your political statement a bad image. What do you think they'll say on TV—two rich, spoiled kids blew up the intake tower at Hoover Dam today. . . ."

"*Shut up!*" Ernesto shouted.

"Maybe she's right," Tiger said. "After all, this is supposed to call attention to poverty. . . ."

"Don't be stupid!" Ernesto cried. He crouched beside Tiger. "Not you, Tiger. It's your sister I meant. She knows nothing about anything. Don't listen to her."

142

"But Tonia's right. I think we should wait for Chief. We can come back and do this another day."

"She's not right!" Ernesto jumped to his feet. "This has nothing to do with poor people—it has to do with your government," he cried. "With your CIA that stick its nose where it don't belong, that put the dictator into power in my country. This is to show that your government, which act so big and strong, is nothing but weak and rotten inside. That your government cannot even protect its big dam from an old man and a small boy. If the old man is not here, so much the better! We will show that one small boy alone can make look like asses the whole security system of this big U.S. dam!"

Two hands crashed onto Ernesto's shoulders, spinning him around. The Hawk had removed his glasses so that his eyes showed, eyes so pale they looked inhuman. Riveting Ernesto with those icy eyes, The Hawk said, "*Silencio!*" When Ernesto tried to protest, The Hawk moved his hand up Ernesto's neck to just beneath the jaw, and began to squeeze with his forefinger and thumb. "*Control!*" he cried.

"Sí. Control!" Ernesto gasped. He coughed after The Hawk released him; his voice was raspy when he spoke to Tiger again. "You see, my friend, what we do will still strike a blow for the poor and oppressed. Your government causes much misery with its . . ." He coughed again. "Imperialistic policies," he continued, rubbing his throat. "In my country . . . my father . . . I told you what the police . . ."

"I understand," Tiger said.

"You do? Then you will go ahead as we planned?"

143

"Yes."

Oh no, I don't believe this, Tonia thought. Tiger can't be doing this, not after all the terrible things Heather told him would happen if he dove in open water!

"Please hurry," Ernesto said, again checking his watch.

"Help me, Tonia."

The heat bore down on them with physical heaviness. "Hurry, I'm dying!" Tiger cried as Tonia fumbled to zip up the dive suit, then pull the hood over his head. She let him lean against her while he put on his fins. Even though the mask hung around his neck so that his nose and mouth were free to breathe ordinary air, Tiger was suffocated by the hundred and twenty degree lake-surface temperature. By the time Tonia lifted the heavy at-pack onto his shoulders, he sagged against the rail. She had to reach around him to fasten the buckle at his waist.

"Get into the water fast, so you'll cool off," she told him.

"No, wait! You forgot the most important thing. The bomb!" Ernesto said.

While Ernesto knelt in front of him and The Hawk came to help, Tonia lifted the air tank to relieve Tiger's shoulders of its weight. The Hawk held the three sticks of dynamite, topped with blasting cap and timer, against Tiger's right thigh; Ernesto tied the bomb in place. One piece of rubber tubing around the top and another near the bottom held the device unslipping against the rubberized material of the dive suit.

"See—no knots in the tubing," Ernesto told Tiger.

144

"You can take it off easily underwater. Now go, and don't waste a second!"

As Tiger lowered himself onto the steps at the stern of the boat, Ernesto kept shouting at him. "You sure you know what to do? Where to go? That tower there. Watch the compass—go straight southwest. A hundred and fifty yards, that's all. We'll wait right here for you."

Tiger put the regulator into his mouth and took a giant step off the boat. As he splashed down, the waters of Lake Mead closed over his head like the gates of a tomb.

Almost instantly he splashed up again, arms raised above his head, fingertips touching. The diver's sign for "okay"! Quickly Tiger pointed to his chest, meaning "me," then made the okay sign again.

"I'm okay," he was trying to tell Tonia, just before he grabbed the diver vehicle and sank beneath the surface.

He's okay. That must mean he isn't going to do it, Tonia thought. But as she watched, a trail of bubbles showed the direction Tiger was taking—straight southwest, toward the intake tower.

145

Twelve

Watching the depth gauge on his console, Tiger descended to twenty feet, then thirty feet, the way Ernesto had instructed him. The intake tower lay a hundred and fifty yards due southwest, and the compass on his console clearly showed where southwest was. He switched on the headlight; it speared a pale blue tunnel through the darker blue around him as the DPV pulled him gently through the water.

He didn't have any way to measure distance, but he judged he'd gone thirty yards when he stopped. That was far enough that the people in the boat should no longer be able to see his bubbles.

Suspended in the water, held up by the inflated balloons in his at-pack, Tiger's body felt weightless. No sound distracted him except the sound of his breathing, and the harsh beating of his heart.

In the dimness of the water, he could not clearly see the bomb tied to his leg, but he felt it. With the same fear and revulsion that a cobra coiled around his thigh would have caused him, Tiger felt that dynamite pressing against his flesh. Instinct made him want to tear it off and throw it away, but if he threw it, it wouldn't go far. Not underwater. The bomb was set to explode in an hour, giving him plenty of time to decide how to dispose of it. That is, if Ernesto hadn't lied about that, too, the way he'd lied about other things.

To call attention to poverty and injustice, he'd said. Hah! Tiger had been suckered like an ignorant baby, believing all that garbage Ernesto fed him. All along, the whole plot was to make the United States look stupid.

Carefully, trying to keep his hand from shaking, Tiger undid the top piece of rubber tubing from his leg. He could work with only one hand, because he had to hold onto the diver's vehicle with the other, so he wouldn't lose it. When the top piece of tubing came loose, it started to float away like a sea worm unwinding, but Tiger was able to grab the end of it.

His breath—audible as bubbles rose from his regulator—became ragged from fear as he slid the dynamite sticks upward, out of the bottom piece of tubing. Now that he no longer believed in Ernesto, he doubted every word the man had ever said. What if the bomb had been set to go off—not in an hour, but that very second?

Tiger moved with such caution that the dimension of time slipped from his consciousness. He climbed astride the DPV like a jockey on a horse. Placing the dynamite between his knees so it wouldn't sink out of reach, he managed to tie the bomb to the nose of the DPV. That was the easiest way to get rid of it—send it off on the DPV.

147

There was one tremendous problem: the DPV wouldn't move unless its power switch was held back in the ON position. Tiger looked for something he could tie the switch with, to lock it back toward the handle.

He'd used both pieces of rubber tubing to fasten the dynamite—he had had to tie both ends, or the bomb would pull loose when the vehicle moved. When he checked every part of his gear, he found nothing else he could use as a cord. Then he saw his watch.

Dad will kill me if I blow up my expensive watch, Tiger thought. He was so scared he didn't realize how ridiculous the thought was.

Wrapping his arms around it so he wouldn't lose it, Tiger slid himself off the DPV and unstrapped his watch. As soon as he buckled the strap in a loop around the handle and the switch, the diver vehicle began to move. Tiger checked his compass and pointed the vehicle northeast. And downward. It would propel itself to the lake bottom, he hoped, and explode against the barren cliffs on the Arizona side of Lake Mead.

A loud noise hit his eardrums with such force he thought the bomb had exploded. But no shock wave hit him. When his panic let up enough for his brain to function, Tiger recognized the sound—a motor boat starting.

It had to be the *Hot Fudge,* because no other boats were in the area. If any had come, he'd have heard them; sound traveled considerably better through water than through air. The motor noise increased in volume until it pounded his temples. Then it began to move away.

Maybe they're turning the boat around or something, he thought. No, the sound kept going farther away.

They were leaving him. Leaving him behind, alone in Lake Mead with a bomb nearby that might or might not reach the empty Arizona shoreline before it exploded. *Leaving him!*

Tiger began to kick his legs as fast as he could, turning himself southwest, churning toward the Nevada side. With the DPV gone, he had no light to see by. He kicked and kicked and kicked, but he didn't seem to move fast at all. In a short time—although he had no way to tell, with his watch gone—he began to tire.

Panic, and Tiger's lack of natural rhythm, made him move inefficiently. He didn't know that, because he didn't even understand rhythm, never having had any. Without a steady, even, rhythmic kick to propel him, he was fighting the water, fighting himself, maximizing rather than minimizing his own surface area. Instead of swimming like a fish, streamlining through the water, Tiger wobbled like a caterpillar on a pine cone.

The cold water began to take its toll; he grew more tired as his body used energy to stay warm. That was even before he hit the thermocline, a pocket of cold water only 54 degrees Fahrenheit. If he'd had the energy to check his thermometer, Tiger would have been surprised that the water temperature had plunged from 85 at the surface to 54 just thirty feet below. But kicking his feet took all the energy he possessed.

His legs grew heavy. Grew stiff. Better get up to the surface, he thought, where the water is warm. He kicked up. Again and again he kicked up. Surely he'd

149

risen thirty feet! Why wasn't the surface there? Was it in a different direction? That way, maybe? If he could find his depth gauge, he'd see how far down he was. But he couldn't remember which of the round dials on the console was the depth gauge.

He was so cold. What was he supposed to keep doing? Oh yeah—breathe. Someone had told him once that it was important to breathe. But what was important about it? Tiger couldn't remember.

.   .   .

Tonia, too, thought they were just turning the boat around when The Hawk started the motor. Even when they'd gone a hundred feet from the buoys, she thought they would turn around and go back.

At two hundred feet she realized they were heading in a straight line—away from the dam.

"What are you doing? Where are you going?" she shouted to Ernesto. He didn't answer.

"Hey! Turn around! We've got to go back and get my brother!"

The Hawk laughed, a terrible sound. He pushed up the throttle, making the boat surge forward even faster.

"Ernesto!" Tonia screamed. "Turn around! Go back!"

This time Ernesto answered. "Too late now."

"What did you say?"

He shouted over the roar of the motor. "There was a chance Tiger might make it, but we wasted too much time getting him into his gear. So now there is no chance for Tiger. The bomb will explode in six minutes. A shame. He was a nice kid, your brother."

"No!" Tonia screamed. "You can't let him get killed!"

"A shame," he said, "because it make lots more trouble. We have to find the old Indian and blame the whole thing on him. Tell everyone it was his plan." Ernesto grimaced. "As if he could think up this clever operation, that stupid old man. When the police find his body, they'll believe he commit suicide from remorse because Tiger died."

"*No! No!*" Tonia's screams sank in her throat as Ernesto moved toward her to stand in front of her. He smiled slightly, almost with satisfaction.

"The only one I won't mind killing," he said, "is you, muchacha of the big mouth. Do you think you could swim from here to shore?"

Numb, she shook her head.

Ernesto grabbed her arms. "Good! Because here is where you go into the water. In the middle of Lake Mead."

As wind whipped Ernesto's black hair around his handsome face, he pushed Tonia hard against the side of the boat, and bent her backward. The rail dug into her back—it hurt! Pain jerked her out of her numb fear. She had to fight!

At first, Tonia struggled while Ernesto held her arms so tightly his fingers bruised her. He shoved, then lifted, trying to force her over the side. But he hadn't counted on Tonia's solid weight. She was heavier than he'd expected.

Suddenly Tonia stopped struggling. She slumped, letting her body become a dead weight. That made it even

151

harder for Ernesto; he put both arms around her to lift her up. With a swift movement, Tonia raised her leg and kneed him, hard, where it would hurt most. Having a brother had taught her certain tactics.

"Ow!" Ernesto roared. He let go of Tonia as he fell and curled like a fetus on the floor of the boat, where he groaned in agony.

The Hawk yelled things that Tonia didn't understand. Keeping one hand on the steering wheel, he reached to help Ernesto up. The moment he took his eyes off her, Tonia lunged. She grabbed the wheel, and gave it a hard yank to the left that caused the boat to turn sharply, making The Hawk lose his balance. Ernesto screamed again as The Hawk landed on him.

Tonia turned the wheel hard right, then hard left, back and forth, one after the other, so the boat bounced in its own wake. Yelling, scrambling, neither Ernesto nor The Hawk could get up. They were tossed from side to side as the boat headed back toward Hoover Dam.

"Imbécile!" Ernesto screamed at Tonia. "I will beat you to death!" But he couldn't beat her if he couldn't get up! Tonia had to keep Ernesto from ever reaching her.

Not far from them, close to the Arizona side, the diver propulsion vehicle skimmed along on the surface, carrying its three sticks of dynamite. At three miles an hour, it headed straight for the *Hot Fudge,* which zigzagged erratically as it edged toward the Arizona side of the lake. The DPV had not stayed submerged, as Tiger intended, because it was designed to float. That

152

way, it couldn't sink and get lost if a diver let it go.

Left! Right! Back and forth, Tonia jerked the wheel. Glancing behind her, she saw that the maneuver wasn't going to work much longer. Ernesto and The Hawk were almost on their feet. They'd grasped benches, handles, the rail, anything they could use for handholds, and had clawed themselves nearly upright.

Finally Ernesto stood up. In awful, gutteral language he told Tonia what he was going to do to her.

"Don't touch me!" she screamed. She clung to the wheel as Ernesto lunged for her.

He never reached her. Before he could, the bomb exploded, only a hundred yards from them.

An orange flash, a roaring blast, then came the shock wave that hurtled Ernesto and The Hawk off the boat. Tons of water lifted into the air and fell back down with enormous force. In the rocky corridor between two state borders, high waves sloshed like water in a dropped bucket as Tonia locked her arms around the steering wheel and hung on for dear life.

First the *Hot Fudge* nosed up, almost out of the water. Then it smacked down hard, with its prow in the water and its propeller churning empty air. As the waves rose and tossed it, the boat rocked violently from side to side.

At any second Tonia expected it to split apart. But the *Hot Fudge* was the most expensive vessel of its size, built to withstand severe storms. It stayed afloat and, miraculously, kept running. At full speed.

"Oh *no*!" Tonia yelled. She was speeding straight for

153

the rocks on the Arizona side. She gave the wheel a full turn, and prayed. Then she was heading for the rocks on the Nevada side.

"I don't know how to stop the dumb thing!" she screeched, although no one was there to hear her. "Where's the brake?" But the boat didn't seem to have a brake. At forty miles an hour, all she could do was steer it in a circle, and hope it would soon run out of gas.

The roar, the speed, the slapping against waves— Tonia felt in the middle of a watery nightmare. She sobbed when she thought of Tiger. Since the bomb hadn't gone off at the intake tower, it might still have been strapped to Tiger's leg when it exploded. Her cries of grief circled the water as the runaway boat left a coiling wake.

On the third orbit she noticed something coming toward her. A rowboat. A white rowboat. She could only take quick glances, because she had to pay attention to her steering.

Someone in the rowboat waved at her. As the boat came closer, she thought it looked like . . . Chief! It was Chief!

Only he wasn't waving. He was holding up his hand to make a sign. With his forefinger and thumb pressed together, as though he were holding something, he rotated his wrist.

What did that mean?

He rotated his wrist again, then pulled it back.

A radio? Was he signing to turn on a radio? If the *Hot Fudge* had one, Tonia didn't know where it was, and she certainly couldn't stop steering long enough to find out.

Turn, pull. Turn, pull. Chief wasn't signing to turn something on, he was signing to turn it *off*! With a key! Turn a key and pull it out!

Tonia made a dive for the boat's ignition key. The key ring had been dangling right in front of her eyes the whole time, and she'd never thought of it. As soon as she snatched it out, the motor died, the propeller stopped, and the *Hot Fudge* settled down into the waves as gently as an inner tube. Tonia burst into tears.

Still blubbering, she ran to the side of the boat to find Chief. She straightened and almost fell over the rail as she got a look into the bottom of the approaching rowboat. Tiger lay there, unmoving, in his diving gear.

"He's unconscious," Chief shouted. "But he's alive." That made Tonia cry even harder, from relief.

Opening Night

"So I hitched a ride to the dam. Then I walked down the road to the lake. That's where I saw the big boom —from the road."

Chief was repeating this story for Bobby Calamity, who'd come backstage to wish him luck on opening night.

"Five minutes!" The announcement carried over the sound system to all the dressing rooms and every part of the stage.

"So what did you do next?" Bobby asked Chief.

"I ran down to the boat house where the Park Service keeps its launch. But I don't know how to drive a launch. Then a big wave from the explosion lifted a rowboat out of the boat house and threw it at my feet, almost. I took that as a sign."

Bobby smiled at Chief's old-fashioned beliefs. "I better get out front," he said. "They gave me a real special seat for tonight, thanks to you, Grandfather. But one more thing I wanna ask—how'd you find Tiger in all the waves?"

Chief answered, "That bright-colored hood he had on, and his yellow hair, floating out in front of it." He looked thoughtful. "You know, yellow hair can be a useful thing. Too bad our people never got any."

In the opposite wing, across the stage, Mona hugged Tonia. "My baby," Mona murmured. "You look absolutely beautiful."

"This black wig makes me look like more of an Indian than Chief does," Tonia answered.

"Two minutes," came the final amplified call. "Cast and crew onstage."

"Look at Tiger," Tonia said as she pointed across the stage. "I've never seen him look so happy."

"He's utterly thrilled," Mona agreed.

Because the newspapers and television had been full of reports about the attempt on Hoover Dam, about Ernesto's death, and about Tonia's and Tiger's part in all of it, Ben Bass decided to put Tiger in the first number. Ben wasn't just taking advantage of free publicity—he felt really proud of Tiger and Tonia.

Dressed in Indian costume, wearing a black wig and brown makeup, Tiger rode bareback on Principe as Don Filipe led the horse onto the stage. Tiger would do nothing except sit on the horse during the whole number, while Principe stood in one spot, but he couldn't have been more blissful if he'd been awarded a gold medal for bravery.

Tiger was really interested in Indians again, and in wanting to help people—the right way. Chief had even taken him to visit the reservation. Tonia couldn't go with them; she'd had a special fitting scheduled with the wardrobe people, so that they could pad her costumes. Much to Ben's dismay, she'd lost more weight.

"Break a leg, honey," Mona whispered in the traditional good-luck wish as Tonia took her position onstage.

A long drum roll, followed by a blare of trumpets, started the live orchestra on a medley of tunes from the show. The music made the hairs on Tonia's arms rise straight up, as though she'd been charged with static electricity. Then, while the orchestra held a long, low chord, a highly amplified male voice announced, "LADies and GENtlemen, the WESTAmerica HOTEL PROUDly prESENTS a DAZzling new reVUE—*The WAY the WEST BeGAN*. With the Buzzy Gutierrez Dancers, the WestAmerican Beauty showgirls, AND . . ."

The curtain rose.

". . . FEAturing the KIDS who SAVED our LIGHTS!— TONIA AND TYLER O'MALLEY!"

Two spotlights switched on, one pointed at Tiger and one at Tonia, as the audience applauded.

Tonia hadn't known they were going to say that. Or turn a spot on her. It caught her by surprise. Batting her long, fake eyelashes, she made a comic-modest face.

A swell of laughter rose from the audience, of far greater volume than she'd ever heard when she was clowning just for the cast. Twelve hundred people sat out there—a full house—and they liked her!

They liked her! A sob caught in Tonia's throat, from the thrill of her first opening night, her first audience. She stole a quick look into the wings, where Mona waited in her flamenco costume.

Mona was crying, but crying carefully so she wouldn't ruin her makeup. Tonia knew that the tears were from joy. They'd made it! Mother and daughter were in a major show together. Mona blew her a kiss.

BOOM boom boom boom . . . The drumbeats for the Indian dance began. Without any direction from her head, Tonia's feet moved in the correct steps. As she shuffled in her circle dance, by herself, stage left, she was able to see into the right wings.

A beaming Casey stood there, on Tiger's side of the stage, to give Tiger moral support. As if he needed any! Chief was there, too, next to Casey. Naturally, Tonia thought. Chief was always on Tiger's side.

Just before the dance ended, she had another chance to glance at Chief.

He'd been watching Tonia, not Tiger. He pointed at her, and gave her a special sign. Thumbs up! Chief's sign of approval.

The applause from the audience was tremendous.

GLORIA SKURZYNSKI decided to write the Mountain West Adventures to acquaint readers with the variety and beauty of her adopted region. From her homebase in Salt Lake City, Utah, the author has fully explored each of the settings for her novels.

Lost in the Devil's Desert takes place near one of her family's favorite camping sites in Utah. *Trapped in the Slickrock Canyon* is about a flash flood in Arizona's spectacular canyonland. *Caught in the Moving Mountains* was written after the author visited the White Cloud Mountains in Idaho. And this latest survival adventure is based on extensive interviews with Las Vegas personalities and a thorough knowledge of Nevada's Lake Mead.

Gloria Skurzynski is particularly pleased that *Trapped in the Slickrock Canyon* has won the 1985 Golden Spur Award from the Western Writers of America; that *Lost in the Devil's Desert* has won the Utah Children's Book Award; and that Mountain West Adventures are currently on the children's book award reading lists in Arizona, Arkansas, Indiana, Iowa, and Missouri.